DOWN BY THE RIVERBANK

Jennifer Odom

The Black Series
Summer on the Black Suwannee
Stranger with a Black Case
Girl with a Black Soul

The Coral Series
Under the Mango Trees
Along the Forgotten Coast

THE CORAL SERIES
BOOK 3

DOWN BY THE RIVERBANK

A NOVEL

JENNIFER ODOM

WordCrafts Press

To all those burdened and grieved by the sins of their forefathers, and to all those who want more than anything to reconcile with family.

And he shall turn the heart of the fathers to the children, and the heart of the children to their fathers, lest I come and smite the earth with a curse.

Malachi 4:6

1

In Carrabelle, Florida, along The Big Bend of Florida's Gulf coast, 89-year-old Allie Bentley stirred from her tormented sleep and broke free from the nightmare. She clasped a shaky hand against her racing heart while she eyed the room and calmed her breathing. With the other hand, she pushed back the quilt and freed her feet to find the floor so she could sit upright.

Below her, soft squares of moonlight lay across the floor. Solid intact boards. She sat there in the quiet and breathed deep, but the pounding in her chest continued.

Thank God. She'd only been dreaming.

But a significant one. Allie knew the difference.

At best, it could only be a warning, but just as the dream had played out, she knew her store with its ancient-pine walls could burn down in minutes.

Allie shuddered. God forbid, the dream was prophetic, the kind that would actually come to pass.

She'd had those before—good ones, however—like the one where her missing granddaughter came through her store's front door. She'd dreamt it twice.

Turned out to be her great-granddaughter.

But prophetic just the same. It came to pass.

Allie's nostrils flared, searching for any hint of smoke, but she picked up nothing more than the scent of musty screens and walls.

She glanced to the bedstead on her right. Across it hung her cane, same as ever. Nothing amiss.

The beadboard walls stood firm around her. No hint of flame. She turned her eyes to the outdated outlet by the antique dresser.

Squinted hard. Nothing there. On top of the dresser sat the familiar stack of *Reader's Digests* in front of their mirrored image. All her surroundings seemed to say, "Everything is fine. You've experienced a bad dream is all."

But the thrumming in her veins would not let up.

The truth remained. Some of her dreams came true…

Beyond her open doorway in this back end of the building hung the quiet darkness.

Unable to rest, she stood upon her homemade cotton rug. A dream like this could not be ignored.

She grappled for her cane and then put it to use as she hobbled through the dark kitchen and the old parlor to the big door that opened into the store. She leaned her cane against the wall, and then like some strange tree-hugger, placed her cheek against the door and ran her hands across its wood and iron fixtures.

As cool as ever. Satisfied, she stood back and lifted the slat that held the door shut. Wood scrubbed over wood as she pulled it wide. Cool air rolled in from the store's mighty interior, along with a hint of ash and smoke from last night's get-together where they'd met around the stove's warmth. And there, chilled in the middle of summer, they'd dried their storm-drenched clothes. Afterward, she'd smothered the fire with customary skill and then retired quite late. Wood stoves were nothing new to Allie.

Across the dusty countertops stretched rectangles of streetlight. But as lovely as this struck her, she tore away her gaze to scour the dark corners, the ceiling, the wire connections…and detected no sign of trouble.

Allie breathed a sigh.

She closed the door, latched it, and then felt her way back through the shadows to her bed.

The mattress remained warm as she climbed in and pulled the quilt to her chin—even during the summer she covered herself. She only hoped her heart and nerves would quiet down and allow her to sleep.

Outside the dusty window screens, the crickets bowed their songs as if nothing had happened. Allie closed her eyes and concentrated on their music.

Perhaps the excitement of last night's get-together with her newly discovered great-granddaughter Coral had caused…

Yes, that's all it was. The excitement and late hours had caused the dream.

Aunt Allie sat bolt upright, shocked awake by a second bad dream. Her heart, like before, thumped like a bunch of racehorses.

Would this night ever end? Her old heart didn't need all this.

Silence now filtered in through the screens, replacing the song of the crickets. The dear little things had all gone to sleep. Thank God, dawn would arrive soon and lift this darkness. It couldn't come soon enough.

Allie's ears perked again as her feet touched the rug.

She rose, took her cane, and stepped to the dresser to retrieve her glasses from their spot atop the *Reader's Digests*.

"Dear Lord," she whispered, "I'm begging. Please don't let this night's dreams be prophetic."

This time, instead of checking the store, Allie crossed the kitchen to the left where her new best friend of all times, Rosella, slept in the adjacent bedroom, along with Coral, the very same great-granddaughter whose recent appearance fulfilled one of Allie's dreams.

This nightmare, like the previous one, demanded Allie check things immediately.

Because in the dream white doves flew down Rosella's arms and out beyond her fingers. What else could the dream mean but death?

Maybe Allie could save her new best friend.

She switched on the kitchen light so she could see into the bedroom without disturbing Rosella and stepped toward the closed door.

The knob trembled in her hand.

2

In Carrabelle, Ralph Stone walked up the west end of the bridge. At this sunny time of morning, it still lay in full shadow. He paused halfway up and smiled. Then just like in his childhood, he thrust his arms up through the sun's rays where they shot horizontally over its crest.

Normally, people wouldn't care about that straight line of the sun. Ralph cared. In school, he knew the basics before they were taught, such as *light travels in a straight line,* and all that. That one he'd learned right here at the bridge.

His first treks over the bridge started at age six and lasted on up into his teen years. Every school day, he'd cross over to Bentley's Store and sit by Aunt Allie's cast-iron stove to wait for the school bus.

And most every day on the bridge, he'd reach up and pierce the flat plane of light with his hands, just like this morning.

He lowered his arms again as long-ago events tumbled before him like chips in a kaleidoscope—things that hijacked his youth— Nadine dropping into his life and hiding like a wounded bird, her evil father's futile armed pursuit, the way it all ended with Ralph and Nadine, Ralph's guilt, his flight into the Army, then his return home upon his father's death—yeah, Ralph deserved that. And with it came the inheritance of that dad-gummed restaurant he never asked for.

His life, like a sinking boat, was sucked below the surface, and there was no way to right it.

How could there be?

Meanwhile, Ralph kept the restaurant open. He gave the business a fair shot, in honor of his dad. But it never flourished.

What more was there for him? If it weren't for that restaurant keeping him afloat, and Millie, his girlfriend, pushing him along, he'd have probably curled up and died somewhere under a bridge.

Until last night.

All because of the news he learned… *Oh, God, thank You!*

Ralph was no killer.

He took a deep breath and ascended the bridge until sunlight hit his face and then consumed his body.

Its brilliance forced his eyes shut. He kept them closed and allowed his fingers to guide him along the rail.

Last night's storm had brought him that news. It washed everything clean.

Nadine had kept their baby. His daughter was alive.

The girl's face, though angry, was so like her mother's—*Thank God Nadine hadn't*—And then how stupid of him to not realize her hate for him before that night. He deserved it. But he couldn't care less. His daughter was alive.

The sun seared Ralph's closed lids as he paused there at the apex to raise his arms like a victor.

And then she'd called him Daddy on top of it. His arms punctuated the thought. Tears burned behind his lids.

He dropped his arms and turned to sit there on the rail, soaking up the warmth, free now, free—from the lead coffin of being a murderer.

Coral was her name. Of all the dear choices, her mother called her Coral. It made perfect sense.

He gripped the rail and thrust an arm into the sky. "Alive! Alive!" he bellowed and laughed aloud. Boaters downriver would think he'd cracked his bean. But Ralph didn't care. He stood now, and repeated, his voice quiet now, even hoarse. "Alive! Alive!"

Her beautiful, angry face simply proof of life. He chuckled at her blast of anger last night. Let the sweet thing yell at him. So what? She was okay. And then a thing he couldn't have hoped for—she forgave him.

He choked then, just to think of it.

Yes, he'd left Nadine the money, but he'd never intended for her to…not really.

And then Nadine left—disappeared before he could tell her—his bad advice echoing in that empty room and following him through the years like a murderer's curse.

Ralph opened his eyes toward the town and the double yellow lines where last night's surprise encounter took place with Coral in the middle of a raging storm.

But as he did, the sight below the bridge stopped him cold. Electrified, he lurched into a sprint, pumping, stumbling, nearly falling down the other side, one foot competing with the other. "Millie!" he gasped, his momentum pulling him along the pavement in seeming slow motion. Street signs and properties flew by as he raced to reach the upended roots, massive trunk, and downed limbs blocking his girlfriend's place.

"Millie!"

I grinned when Matt Flores, the love of my life, settled beside me on the ancient steps of Aunt Allie's back porch.

"Coral," he said and leaned in with a warm kiss. "You all right this morning?"

He gathered up my hand and cupped it between his.

My other hand cradled the green frog clicker, the very catalyst that led me to follow my dad and confront him out in the middle of the highway last night. He didn't even realize I was his daughter.

"How am I?" I answered. "Ever have ice water poured over you? In a happy way, I mean."

Matt opened a hand for me to hand him the clicker. "I know the feeling."

I handed the gadget over. He'd seen it laying around on top of Aunt Allie's post. To everyone else it was her *chicken clicker*. She used it to call the chickens in to eat and then locked them up for the night. It had a different meaning for me. And when the time was right, I'd explain to him. But now wasn't the time.

"Truth can be that way," he said.

I pinched two fingers together. "I was this close to not telling him I'm his daughter."

He smiled. "And then you listened to the rest of his story."

I leaned away. "Am I detecting an *I told you so?*"

He laughed and hugged my shoulders. "Yeah, well, just a little, Miss Beautiful-but-Stubborn. However, I'm glad things turned out for you the way they did."

No doubt I could be hard-headed. Matt and Zeke, his boss and owner of the fishing charter boat, the *Gulf Princess,* had begged me to hear the rest of my dad's story. But my mind was made up after the first half. And that placed Matt in a precarious position when I insisted in a very firm tone that he drop the subject. But I should have listened to him.

"You were right," I conceded. "Absolutely right."

I sighed and gazed down at the clicker in his hand. "Thanks for trying."

When my dad showed up at Aunt Allie's, my anger had exploded. If I hadn't practically chased him out to the middle of that highway to tell him off, I wouldn't have learned that he'd actually wanted me—his child—my entire life. Twenty wasted years.

And I almost cast him aside—to spend the rest of my days as the supposed end of my family line—such as it was.

Poor Mama, she did the best she could, I guess—God rest her soul.

"I've been thinking," I said.

"Uh oh." He dropped his head as if I were going to scold him. Of course, I had been irritated with him, and he knew it, but not that irritated.

I elbowed him with a laugh. "Come on, now, drama guy."

He fake-mopped his brow. "Whew! Skin of my teeth."

"—but I did consider wringing your neck, along with Zeke's yesterday."

He grabbed his neck as if he were choking and pretended to fall over. "Nooooo!"

I gave his arm a shake. "You silly rabbit." After all the recent stress it was good to laugh. I waited for him to compose himself. "Okay, seriously now…"

Besides the good news about my father last night, I'd discovered something else. The friend that Rosella and I called Aunt Allie was actually my great-grandma.

"There's a gap in my history, Matt—wider than the Grand Canyon—and Aunt Allie's eighty-nine years old. *Eighty-nine.*"

Matt nodded.

I had one semester left before college graduation, and so did Matt. "There's family history to catch up on. Think about it. If I go back to school in North Carolina right now, she might be gone when I get back. What's more expedient? School can wait."

He shrugged. "I know."

I spread my hands. "How could I justify leaving?"

"Good point."

"And then there's my dad—even more to learn—I've never even had a step-father."

Matt waited, allowing me to finish.

I slumped against his shoulder. "It's all so overwhelming."

He nodded and patted my knee. "You'll do just fine."

His sincerity encouraged me.

Selfishly, I wished Matt could stay and see me through it all. But I said nothing. He needed to finish his last quarter and graduate.

Of course, Carrabelle wouldn't be the same without Matt. I would have to brace myself.

"Thank you, Matt. Thank you for coming up here, for being here for me."

He cupped my chin, and his dark eyes looked into mine as he kissed me for the second time. "I wouldn't have it any other way. I love you. You know that, don't you?"

My heart did a pirouette, and I smiled, but my eyes burned.

He leaned away, and I blinked and gave him a nod. "And I love you. So much," I whispered.

The third kiss lasted a little longer, and he gathered my hands in his. "I'm not going anywhere, Coral. Not with things as they are. We'll pray our way through it all. Look how far God's already brought you—brought us."

Of course, prayer…

And yes, God had brought me far, rescued this endangered child from the worst trailer in the trailer park, a neglectful mother, and a life connected by mere threads to this—Matt didn't know the half of it. I scrunched my eyes shut. *Oh, God, I thank You.*

Wait.

I opened my eyes and straightened. "Shouldn't you be at work? No charter boat today?"

Matt was Zeke's temporary hire while the deckhand was healing up from a nasty shark bite. Matt had taken a job so he could be productive while in town and save Grandma some rent money. He could never be called lazy.

He opened his palm and examined the clicker. "Cancelled."

Of course, the storm last night.

Well, goody. I'd have him to myself today.

I watched his face as he studied the steps below his feet, and I wondered what else was on his mind. Day by day, I watched his skin grow darker and darker from being out on those waters. He never burned. Cuban blood.

He grinned down at me. Those brown eyes melted me.

"Don't go by looks." Grandma Rosella would always say, "Go by character."

Well, ignoring Matt's looks was no easy task. He was tall, dark, and handsome—but most of all, kind. Like his Grandfather Eduardo.

Grandfather Eduardo's wife, Rosella, wasn't my real grandma, but I loved her like one. We were neighbors in the trailer park, and she'd taken me under her wing at age twelve before Mama died.

Funny, though, Rosella never showed me her grandson Matt's picture. Or talked much about him. Or let on when she paid my college tuition to a school in North Carolina—and his as well. Perhaps she hoped we'd bump into each other naturally.

Our paths never crossed until a few weeks ago when we met at the office of Peter Cordero, our family lawyer.

Grandma Rosella had to know I'd be smitten. And I was.

"Two grandmas," I said. "Wonder what I should call Aunt Allie."

Matt shrugged.

"You know, she woke up in a bit of a tizzy this morning," I said.

"Told me to be very careful in the kitchen because she had some nightmare about the store burning down."

Matt frowned and gazed down at the gadget.

Eventually he cleared his throat. "Well, on another note—I've got some news of my own," he said.

I turned his way.

"What do you choose first, light news or heavy news?"

I had no idea.

Matt shifted on the steps. "Great, then. Light news it is…Millie lost her oak tree."

"Lost?"

"As in fell over," he said, acting it out with his arm.

"Is sh…?"

"She's fine. You didn't hear the noise?" He flung his hands apart. "*Blam!* Shook the whole place. Sounded like a dump truck hitting a wall."

"I'm surprised I didn't hear it," Coral said.

"Well, with your bedroom on the opposite side of the store, no wonder. Aunt Allie didn't mention hearing it?"

Coral shook her head and reached for his hand. "C'mon, show it to me. Let's walk over there."

"Wait, wait." Matt motioned her back to the steps and patted the wood. "Before we do that… Two things."

Coral pretended to pout as she sat back down.

He chuckled but then grew serious. "So—part one," he said. "Peter called."

Anytime Peter got involved, things could get pretty sobering. Peter Cordero was a lawyer and close family friend of Grandma Rosella. He's the one who'd researched Coral's father and ran background checks. Then, finding nothing of concern, he encouraged the three of them to come to Carrabelle and check him out from a distance. If Coral wanted to meet him, fine. If not, then fine as well. But Peter was the cause for them coming up here. Grandma Rosella Flores refused to stay home but needed time to rest from her recent illness. Matt came mainly for both of them, especially for Coral's moral support. How could they send her off alone?

"Dad showed up at Peter's office," Matt continued. "And now he's headed this way."

"Oh boy," Coral said.

Matt's father, Sol Flores, was a pretty angry guy.

"You know he's afraid to fly," Matt said. "After that long drive from Las Vegas, and not finding Grandma in Ft. Myers, he's had to backtrack—so look out. I expect Dad to be extra hateful when he arrives."

Short, balding, and fair-haired, Dad was unlike the rest of his family. He was nasty and self-centered. So many times, his loud abusive voice came through the walls at home when Dad was talking to Grandma Rosella. Matt shuddered to think of his arrival any day now, *to check on his mother's health.* Actually, he probably expected her to be dying.

Coral's face showed concern. "Matt, I don't want him to badger us about that co-executorship thing regarding her will."

Grandma had assigned it to the two of them to keep Dad from taking undesirable liberties with her burial. Neither Coral nor Matt knew anything about it until Peter arranged for the two of them to meet in his office during this semester break. And neither had met until that day they arrived at Grandma's in Fort Myers.

And that's the exact moment Matt fell in love.

He hugged Coral's shoulder. "Don't worry. I won't let him near you."

"What are we going to do? We can't let him harass Grandma. He'll attack her, too."

Matt sucked in a breath and let it out. "Rest assured, that's not going to happen."

Matt would do what was necessary to keep his dad at bay.

He brought his hand up to the crown of Coral's light brown hair and stroked its long waves. This was the girl of his dreams, the kind of woman he never thought he'd find, with all the attributes of his wise grandmother and all the beauty of a princess.

The one he'd want to spend the rest of his life with.

And Dad was not going to destroy it. Not if Matt had anything to do with it.

3

I sat there on the steps and stared across the highway at the lovely masts and furled sails of the quiet harbor as I mulled over the news about Matt's dad. What loud destruction would he bring to the peace and serenity of our little Carrabelle? I shuddered at the thought of it.

Matt seemed to read my feelings and pulled me up by the hand. "It's going to be all right. I'm always here with you, and I'll never leave. And I won't let him pick on you. Now, let's go see that tree."

My dread had distracted me from the tree.

"So, are you ready for the rest of the news?" he said as we came around the side of the store.

I'd forgotten about that, too. "That other was bad enough."

"It's good, really. My mother called me. Actually, a couple of times lately."

"Paulette?"

"Remember what I told you? My mom and dad never married?"

I nodded. She left when Matt was sixteen. It dealt him and his dad a low blow those four years ago, all about the same time Grandpa Eduardo died in Ft. Myers. I'd wondered why they never attended the funeral, but Matt had filled me in. They were simply too distraught.

"It wasn't right what she did. I was her kid. She did me wrong when she just walked away." He paused there in front of the store and gazed toward the water without seeing it.

I took his hand. "Oh, Matt. I can't even imagine that. I-I just have no words." I couldn't blame Paulette for leaving Sol, of course. He was so hateful. But to leave her child?

Even my mother, Nadine, with all her faults, never walked off and left me.

He gazed down at the clicker in his hand. "And now she's asked forgiveness."

I had no doubt Matt would do the right thing. After all, she *was* his mother.

For years, Grandma Rosella and I had prayed for Sol. But I'm ashamed to say, I never once thought about praying for Paulette.

"I know you'll do what's best." I pulled his hand close. "And I'll be right here beside you."

"Like you mentioned before—it's like getting splashed with ice water," he said. "I'm feeling that too. Big time."

"I know. Buckets."

Millie had just zipped up her waitress dress when her cabin's front door burst open.

"Millie!" Ralph seemed frantic.

She poked her head through the bedroom door.

He leaned in, gripping the knob, his face ashen.

Then it occurred to Millie. He must have seen that fallen tree out front.

"Are you okay?" he said.

She smoothed her hem and stepped into the kitchen. "Well, come on in. Good grief. Doesn't anybody knock anymore?"

Ralph motioned toward the cabin's front yard as he stepped inside. "Did you see that thing?"

She laughed as if to say, *how could I miss it?* Its trunk and leafy mass filled her entire lot and part of the street between her place and Aunt Allie's store. Of course, she had.

From the street, it eclipsed the view of Millie's three cabins, but not a leaf had grazed them. She stepped over and gave him a peck on the lips. "I love it that you care enough to worry."

He pulled her close and wrapped his arms around her, smoothing her hair. "Thank God you're okay." He leaned away. "You are, aren't you? I don't know what I'd do if…"

She smiled and reached around him to shove the door closed.

"It fell way after the storm last night," she said. "I was sound asleep, and this loud *craaack* and *pop* woke me right up. I looked around the room, tryin' to figure out what was going on. And before I could sit up, there was a *swoosh*, and a *foom!* Sounded like an elephant falling. Even the windows rattled. I thought the world was comin' apart, Ralph."

He frowned.

"So I grabbed a flashlight and stepped outside to see what happened. And there out of nowhere stood this gigantic new hedge. You saw it. When you came in."

Ralph studied her.

"When I looked up, there came Matt with his own flashlight, squeezin' round it from the left. Boy, was I glad to see him." Matt rented Millie's cabin number two. "We teamed up and checked things over."

"You shoulda…"

Her hand shook as she gestured toward the coffeepot. "Have a cup. It's fresh." She paused. "'Course, the way you came bustin' in here like some kind of wild man, maybe you don't need caffeine."

She knew he hadn't missed her shakiness, but she couldn't control it.

Like a gentleman, he didn't focus on that but glanced toward the coffeepot.

"Shoot," Millie said, "my beautiful tree's gone. Gone." She returned to what Ralph had started to say. "Now, Ralph, really. The tree was already down. Why would I call you and wake you up from a good sleep for that?" She reached up and squeezed his chin. "Not after all you had going on last night."

She turned and stepped toward the coffeepot. Her hand refused to steady as she lifted her own cup off the counter and took a sip. She didn't normally tremble like this. "Rotten trunk, I'm sure of it."

"I would have come right down here, and you know it. You should have called. Next time…you call me anyway. Okay?"

She gave him a quick nod, afraid the rest of herself might fall to pieces like her hands.

"I'm okay, Ralph. That's what counts. Matt's okay. Nobody was hurt. And I love that you care, honey."

Ralph, focused and serious, gathered her in his arms again and gave her a long hug. He held on tight until her shaking stopped—shaking she didn't even know she had until now.

Her nerves finally calmed, and she pulled away. "I'm okay, Ralph, I am." But her knees weren't. "Thank you, honey. I'll just sit down here a minute." Her energy suddenly drained, she scooted out a chair from her red fifties' dinette set and sank down upon it. "Woo. I'm not sure what just happened there." She wrapped both hands around her cup and held it on the table. "Go on ahead and get you some coffee, honey. And then we'll go."

He leaned down to kiss her ever so gently and then stepped over to the pot. He pulled his favorite red mug from the hook over the sink and poured it half full. A special cup from when he used to stay at Millie's. Its gold lettering said *My Man.* Something Millie had special-ordered for him. She liked pretty things in her house, and she liked them to match, and he would always be her man. Even if he didn't want to get married. One could only hope.

His moving out was recent. After Millie had sat in on Aunt Allie's Bible studies, she'd taken the high road and told him to move back into his own place. He pouted and sulked. But once he'd figured out Millie wasn't trying to break up with him, they remained an item.

Ralph stood at the sink sipping his coffee and thinking about who-knows-what.

"Say, did you really mean all what you said last night," she asked, "or were you just a little half-crazed in that storm?" She'd finally figured out—after Ralph and Coral's loud back and forth hullabaloo in the middle of the road—who Coral was. The girl was his daughter. And all his strange behavior around the girl had nothing to do with romantic notions for the twenty-year-old but was him simply tryin' to figure out why she looked familiar.

"Every word of it, sweetheart."

She lifted her near-empty cup like a toast and smiled. "Give me a minute," she said and stood. Steadier now, she stepped back into the bedroom to put on her shoes.

When she came out, she brought her empty cup. He'd downed his coffee as well, rinsed his cup, and set it in the sink. She reached out to set hers beside his, but it slipped and fell against it instead. The shatter of broken ceramic filled the kitchen.

She clapped her hand over her mouth. "Oh, Ralph! I'm so sorry." He had to be disappointed. These were their special cups.

But Ralph shook his head. "It's okay." He took her hands and pulled her toward him. "Accidents happen."

"I'll order us some more."

"Listen, you're rattled this morning. After all, last night was a big night. Don't worry about it."

Millie slipped loose. "We better go." She waved toward the sink. "I can clean that up tonight."

Ralph ignored her and gathered up the chunks of ceramic. He dropped them into the trash and brushed off his hands. "Don't give it another thought."

As she took a deep breath, she thought back to Ralph's words from last night. She paused. This seemed like a good time to make sure she heard them right. "Ralph, about last night, just to be clear, you said I could decorate the restaurant to my heart's content?" It hadn't been all that long since she showed Ralph her ideas, and he'd shut her down.

His grin told Millie all she needed to know.

She glanced at the clock and grabbed her keys. "Okay, then." It was her turn to grin. "We really need to get going. Larry's down at the restaurant by himself." Along with Jack the dishwasher who could barely cook. Jack was catching on, though. And Larry was learning new skills fast. But just the two of them? No. That could be a disaster.

Ralph took the keys from her hand and guided her out the door, locking things up. Still, she couldn't help but wonder why Ralph was out and about on this side of the bridge this morning instead of down at the Captain's Table, his restaurant. He never ever did that.

As they stepped away together and he reached for her hand, it reminded her of one more thing. "Does this mean we can go out together to hunt down the decorations?"

He gave her hand a squeeze and a quick smile.

But the quick fade of his smile and the accompanying sigh told Millie he was probably realizing it was time to bite the bullet and hire her some more wait help. The very thing she'd pressed and pressed him for.

Up until yesterday he'd been dodging her every request.

How quickly life could change.

4

Ralph squeezed Millie's hand. Here was his woman worrin' about decoratin' the restaurant…and he had so much more on his mind beyond that. Last night's revelation of his daughter had changed everything. He sighed at the magnitude of it all and then smiled at Millie. "Like I said, decorate to your heart's content. Make a list, and we'll go hunt the decorations together."

Millie had once shown him her notebook of decorating ideas to enhance the business at his seafood place. He'd discouraged her, even hurt her feelings about it. And for that, he was sorry.

She tugged his hand. "A date?"

She'd often complained they never did things together. But that was about to change.

He gave her a sideways glance. "Sure, baby. A date." And that would give him an excuse to head up to Tallahassee and find her a nice diamond. The very thing she'd hinted about for so long. Like she had always suggested, her body-clock was ticking.

Well, so was his.

Life was too short for all this monkey business.

He turned back long enough to catch a parting glimpse of Aunt Allie's store, where he was first headed this morning.

His heart-to-heart talk with Aunt Allie would have to wait.

Besides, he didn't exactly know how to explain things, on the why and how of Nadine's story—and how much to leave out.

Ralph thought back to that black night when old Horace Smith, Nadine's father, came stomping through the town with his gun. He stopped at every door. "Where's my blasted daughter?" Every other word was a cuss word or God's name in vain. "Whoever's

18

got her, you'll pay for it if you're hidin' her in there. Turn her over to me. Where is she?"

Seeing how Aunt Allie was Nadine's maternal grandmother, Ralph was sure Horace had found his way to her store first. More than likely, he'd spoken as disrespectfully to her as to the other townsfolk.

And that's why Nadine didn't go to Allie Bentley's house.

With the facts out in the open now, Ralph was ready to learn the details concerning her family.

Aunt Allie learned the truth about Ralph last night, that Ralph was Coral's father, so she could certainly piece two and two together and know his relationship with Nadine.

Aunt Allie would have questions.

And she deserved answers, but thank God, she hadn't quizzed him last night. Not on such a happy occasion. Why destroy it?

Nadine's running away—and him hiding her—nobody knew a thing about it, nobody but Zeke, his best buddy from childhood.

And based on Nadine's story, Ralph realized he'd saved her from a fate worse than death or death itself.

And he was pretty sure Aunt Allie knew nothing about what Nadine's father did to Nadine's mother, or to Nadine, or about the baby Nadine lost before she met Ralph. Her father was an incestuous and violent man.

Ralph didn't blame Nadine for running away. Not at all.

At least she was lucky enough to end up on Ralph's doorstep, a young stranger who believed her story and was willing to help.

On the other hand, as heroically as Ralph began, when one thing had led to another over time, it ended differently, and Ralph turned into a complete jerk. He had some serious apologies to make.

There was no excuse for him waiting twenty years to confess his guilt to Aunt Allie. Despite keeping his anonymous eye out for her and helping her in so many ways over the years, he'd studiously avoided her.

How could he face her?

As for the raw facts, Ralph would have to hold some of it back from her.

Not because he didn't owe her the truth, but at her age, if he laid it all out for Aunt Allie, it would likely destroy her.

As well as Coral.

After they arrived at The Captain's Table, Millie parted ways with Ralph and headed straight toward Larry on the other side of the room to retrieve her order pad. Larry shouldn't have to wait tables.

The Captain's Table was jam packed. Of all days! Before she reached Larry, who hadn't noticed her, he finished up his order and delivered it to the kitchen window like a relay racer, picking up two plates for a return to the tables. She nodded her approval. The bumbling teen was highly competent when he needed to be.

She hurried toward him. "I've got it now, honey. Good job," she said as he approached.

Millie eyed the plated toast and eggs in his hands. The food looked pretty decent. So, back in the kitchen, Jack the dishwasher had to be doing okay as well. Who knew? "Ralph's here, too. You get on back to the kitchen and help out your buddy."

She made a mental note to ask Ralph to give them both a little extra pay this week. Just for being so responsible.

Larry delivered the plates, gave her a wordless sigh of relief, and shoved the order pad into her hands as he passed. He plunged back through the double swinging doors.

Ralph had also disappeared into the kitchen, and the crowded restaurant was quickly brought under control. She let the customers know they'd been a little short-handed and asked for patience. "We'll getchall set here in a few minutes," she said.

Back at the order window, Ralph had already slid another pair of plates onto the ledge.

She caught his eye. "Ralph…"

He waved a consoling hand in her direction. "You got it, Millie. The first applicant I see gets the job. The first one."

"The first one?"

"I don't care who it is," he said. "I'm gettin' you some help."

She raised her brows and smiled as she turned away with her pair of plates.

Wow. This change in her man was hard to believe.

But as she wound her way through the dining room, she wondered again what Ralph was doing on her side of the bridge just now instead of back at the restaurant.

5

At lunchtime, the day after the storm, I parked the Mustang in front of The Captain's Table, my dad's restaurant, and helped Grandma Rosella out. I situated her walker so she could grab hold. She frowned at it. "Oh, pshaw. If you're with me I don't really need that thing, do I?"

I smiled and nodded. So many times, I'd wished she were my real grandma. I even hinted as a child once that she adopt me as her grandchild. But it never happened.

Though it grieved me at the time, God knows the better plan for each one of us, and only now that I'd met Matt could I begin to understand.

"We've got rocks to navigate," I said, "and if you end up falling on them, heaven help us. It's not going to be very pretty with you and me wallowing around on the ground with bloody knees. Is it?"

This tickled her funny bone, and she feigned a swat at me.

I helped her through the gravel in the parking lot and up to the door. I held it open for her. "Everything's like new this morning," I said, stepping in behind her. "And after last night, nothing could drive me away from Dad's restaurant."

She took my hand and pressed it against the walker. "I know, honey. I know. And I'm so happy for you." She looked me in the face as another thought changed her visage. "I realize you're in the middle of learning this, but always choose the high road and forgive. It'll take you a lot farther in life."

I agreed. "You know, I almost failed the test."

She grinned. "You came pretty close."

What a change that would have made. This morning wouldn't

be happening. I'd have left this town and dragged a load of hate along with me.

Ralph, my dad, had sorrowed for the last twenty years, thinking I was dead and that he'd caused it. Truth was, he'd never wanted that. What a waste of his life. And mine.

I closed the restaurant door as the cool air of the dining room enveloped us.

I wish I'd known about Dad. After all the stuff Mama put me through, I might have chosen to run away and come up here.

All those years, it never once occurred to me that I might have a living dad. I just assumed whoever he was, he'd died or hopped on a motorcycle and headed off to another city.

Even before Mama died, Grandma became my shining light. When she got sick this last semester, and I nearly lost her forever, I'd found Mama's old letter in her purse. And from that letter I learned I actually had a father. A *mess,* Mama had called him.

But he wasn't.

I placed a hand on Grandma's shoulder and indicated the table to the left. "This is where Matt and I like to sit. Want to try it?"

She led the way and picked the far side of the booth to slide in. I stashed her walker near the register.

Looking back, I realized Mama was the mess.

Through all those years I thought I was the last one of my family line.

Then Peter Cordero, good old Peter, Grandma's family lawyer, located my dad in Carrabelle. And Dad's the one who clued me in to Aunt Allie, who turned out to be my real great-grandma.

"Your head is in the clouds today." Grandma said, taking my hand. "Penny for your thoughts."

I grinned. "Lots to review. Lots to think about."

"I can only imagine."

"I wish Aunt Allie had come with us this morning," I said. "I asked her, but she said, 'Before that happens, Ralph's got to come down here. He owes me a little *tête-à-tête* first.'"

Grandma gave a slow, understanding nod. "I'd sure like to be a fly on the wall."

"Me too. But I wouldn't hold my breath for that invitation," I said. "It could be quite delicate."

Grandma Rosella grinned and poked her menu across the table at me. "You know, you'd better figure out what you're going to call her. She's your great-grandma."

I laughed. "I know. I'll have to ask what she prefers."

Millie stopped by the table and dropped off the menus. "Mighty fine mornin' to you ladies." She shook her head. "What a night, huh? Takes my breath away."

"It's a heart full," was all I could think of in response.

Millie stepped back with her hands clasped under her chin. I wondered if she felt as overwhelmed as I did. Even after the sweet get together around the fire last night. What a way to celebrate all these revelations, sitting around that stove in the old store. It was so much to digest. "I'll be back when you're ready," she said. "Take your time."

Grandma turned back to me. "I can't advise you," she said. "But Great-grandma Bentley is a mouth full of syllables."

I raised my eyebrows. "I like GG. Sounds easy, but it might be too modern. Then there's Grandma Bentley."

Grandma Rosella took my hand. "One thing's for sure, though. And I'd like this very much. You can still call me Grandma."

"Awww," I said. "I'll always call you that." It warmed me to know the old title still mattered to her.

She patted my hand and with a deeply pleased expression, gathered up her menu.

Ralph glanced up as Millie brought another double order to his kitchen window.

"Your daughter's here," she said.

"Great. I was hoping she'd stop in today."

"Betcha can't keep her away now."

He glanced over his shoulder toward the grill. "Larry!" he yelled. "Step over here, son, and fill these orders."

Without delay, Ralph hustled through the double swinging doors and down the hallway to the back door. He had a little something for his daughter.

He reached for the paper bag he'd stashed above the washing machine and checked its contents. *Yep. All there.*

He returned to the register with the bag in hand and paused to remove his soiled apron, mainly because he didn't want to embarrass his daughter, and then headed toward the table where she sat with her Grandma Rosella—not her real grandmother, he'd come to learn. And there was some history there he didn't understand yet, but one day he'd find out.

The women turned and greeted him as he approached. "Good morning, ladies. Do—do you mind if I sit a minute? I have a little something for Coral." He still wasn't certain of how to interact with her today.

Things could have changed between last night and this morning.

Coral scooted over, and he slid in beside her.

The awkwardness of how to speak to his own daughter loomed large. Sure, he was confident around teens like Larry that he mostly hollered at. Matt too, just another guy. But all that was spoken and confessed out in the middle of the highway last night seemed like a dream right now by the light of morning. A sliver of doubt about whether Coral's positive feelings would remain the same after a good night's sleep crept over him. He wanted to step lightly. Not lose her. He hoped he didn't come across as a total doofus or disappoint her by being an idiot. "We had a lot of excitement last night, huh?" he said.

"Oh, my, what a time," Miss Rosella said. "And that fallen tree. Dear me!"

"For sure," Coral said.

Ralph swallowed. Coral might not be much of a morning talker. But she was still speaking. He'd better just dive in. He gripped the bag and set it on the table and opened its folded top. "It's the coral I promised you last night."

"Oh, that's right," Coral said, leaning back.

He reached into the bag. "I knew you'd like to have this. Your mom had a couple of seashells, too. They're in there. Real pretty ones. Whelks, I think."

The ladies watched as he carefully set the coral and the two shells out on the table.

Coral leaned in and touched them with her fingertips. "Oh, they're beautiful."

"My goodness, look at the coral," Miss Rosella said. "No wonder she named you like she did. They're as delicate as fine china."

"I heard they're even more amazing when they're alive," Ralph said. "But I've not been snorkeling. This coral's from down in the Florida Keys."

Ralph decided less was more this morning, so he slid back out of the booth and stood. "Well, I'm glad you like them. But I'd better get back to work now."

"Thank you, Ralph," Miss Rosella said.

"They're gorgeous Daddy, and thank you for saving them for me all these years."

Ralph smiled. *Daddy.* She'd called him Daddy again.

All was well.

"I'll be back with your order."

When he returned with the orders that Larry had piled extra high, he noticed the ladies had placed the coral and shells back into the bag and rolled it shut again. Coral slid something off the table as he approached and held it between two fingers. "You're not going to believe what came out of one of the sea-shells," she said.

He set the plates down and crossed his arms. "Yeah?" Sand or smaller shells frequently got caught in a larger one. He played along. "So, you found something?"

"I did. We heard something rattling around in one of the shells…"

He shifted his weight, rubbed his chin.

"I gave it a bit of a shake. Nothing happened. So I shook it again. And then this." She opened her hand. "This fell out."

He leaned away, his mouth agape.

In her land lay a small gold coin.

Back in the kitchen Ralph worked at the fryer as he contemplated

Coral's gold coin. A sizzle rose as he dumped a new batch of fries into the grease.

He hadn't known what to say when Coral showed him her discovery. He'd tamped down his shock and congratulated her as if it were just another day and another coin. "Take good care of that," he'd told her. "It's a nice keepsake." He'd reached out to examine the coin himself and then handed it back. The engraving was American, not Spanish, as on things found in old shipwrecks. Good, she'd probably be keeping it then.

"It might be a tenth of an ounce," he told her, "and last time I looked it would have been worth about a hundred fifty dollars or so." He'd have to check again. Values evolved throughout the years.

He stared into the sizzling oil as he considered the facts. The shell where Coral found the coin was a shell he'd given to Nadine. Found it himself. Washed and rinsed both the shells. He certainly would have noticed a coin rattling around inside one. And it would have fallen out in the water.

Nadine must have hidden the coin in there.

He grimaced to know the broken state of mind Nadine must have suffered to have left so abruptly—to forget her coral, the shells, this coin—when she had nothing else to her name but the money he stupidly left her.

He bowed his head. *God forgive me,* he said for the gazillionth time.

The fryer's timer beeped, and he blinked hard a few times, lifting the basket of fries and dumping them onto a plate.

Good for Coral that she'd found the coin.

But finding a treasure wasn't the point at all.

The real question was, where would Nadine have gotten a coin like that?

6

After I finished eating, I tucked the gold coin in my change purse and left Grandma at the table while I headed over to the register. Millie, around the corner in the other dining room, had made herself scarce and let my dad wait on us today. Probably so I could see more of him. That was thoughtful of her.

My dad caught me standing there and came out of the kitchen. He slid behind the register and leaned his elbows on the counter.

"What are you doin' tryin' to pay?" His gentle voice reminded me of the way he'd interacted with the kittens behind his restaurant. "Listen, honey, all meals are on me from now on."

I thanked him.

He stepped to the side of the register and hesitated.

"Could I come around there and—do you mind if I give you another hug?"

Last night, he'd hugged me big time in the middle of the road. Picked me up, even. But this was still something new to me, getting hugged by a father figure, and I guessed he sensed it. All Mama's friends were lechers.

I mustered up a little nod.

"I mean—I don't want to be—presumptuous, you know." He opened his arms and for an instant, I thought of those movies where Italians give out lots of hugs.

I smiled, and we traded a quick hug. He patted my back, and I almost laughed as I imagined him saying, *Atsa gooda girl,* like some big Italian guy. Now that I'd accepted him as my dad, I'd try not to hold back my hugs, but this was new, and I'd have to get used to it. "We appreciate the lunch today," I said.

He stood back. "It's all right. It's all right." He paused as if he were trying to think of something else to say.

At the same time, I was hoping for a good lead-in to ask him one more question. More of a favor.

He finally came up with, "You ladies have any big plans today?"

I shifted my purse onto my shoulder. "Zeke's charter got cancelled, so Matt and I are going to hang out."

"That's good. You tell him I said to behave himself," he said, and laughed. "No, seriously, Matt's a fine young man."

I agreed and realized this was my chance. "I do have an important favor to ask, though."

His eyebrows rose. "And what might that be?"

I braced my arm on the counter. "Would you be willing to take me out to Mama's place?"

"You mean…?"

I nodded. "Where she lived."

He stepped back. It seemed to me like he was thinking, *Man, oh, man, that's not a good idea.*

I waited.

He tipped his head back and took on a pained expression. He rubbed his cheeks. I could tell he wanted to say no, but he was trying to be nice. "I might need to think on that one, honey."

I let it go for the time being. At least he hadn't said no. But my heart felt like lead as we said our good-byes and headed out. Maybe soon I'd ask him again.

I didn't want to pester him, but I had to know more about my family. As far as I knew, he was the only person alive who could help me.

Ralph remained at the register as the restaurant's door closed behind Coral and her Grandmother Rosella. He frowned and tried to think back twenty years to Nadine's directions of how to get down there to her dad's old place, an old squatter's camp he'd built. A place to hide from his past.

Whatever that was.

Ralph and Nadine had spoken of it several times. She drew it out once, on a brown paper bag, and he'd planned to remember it, for future reference. But that was twenty years ago.

The place was well-hidden, down in Tate's Hell, part of a State Forest now and watched over by the Forestry Service. Not a place where Ralph wanted to go poking around, not then, not ever. Never mind the old legends.

The family squatted in an unused area that no one—not in their right mind—would ever access.

Aw, dang, what had Nadine told him? Something about a stand of trees—that's it, sister palms—a grandaddy cypress tree. And there was a spring.

He drummed his fingers on his chin, remembering. Five steps. He remembered that. Cross over, and go a mile up creek until *the water ripples over a three-point rock…*or was it two miles? Then something about *orchids* on the left or right. The flow of the creek, the plants, that could all change.

He crossed his arms. This was ridiculous. A needle in a haystack.

But Coral was his daughter. And she'd asked.

He tried to picture the route Nadine drew—back when he was young and stupid and had considered vengeance on Nadine's dad because of what he'd done to her.

The map was long gone. And now, how in the heck could he even be sure? He might identify a camp like hers if he saw it, but a lean-to of branches and palm logs would have rotted away years ago. Twenty years would decimate soft wood.

Could be remnants, though. Artifacts.

If he took Coral—no, he couldn't. Not before he went and found it for himself.

For his sake and hers, he hoped Nadine's old man was long gone.

Because he'd certainly be taking his pistol.

7

I stood by the back steps of the store as Matt pulled the Mustang around and climbed out. As he snapped the door shut, he winked over the roof at me.

"I'll take the backseat," I said.

"What, you don't want to drive?"

I had to laugh. There was no way Aunt Allie could get into the backseat. And though I liked the Mustang, I wasn't about to drive.

It was so great that Matt and I could hang out today. Earlier, while he showed me the downed tree, he suggested this ride with Aunt Allie so she could show us the area where she'd spent most of her life. "We all know car rides are a great time to chat," he said, "and I want to hear everything she has to say."

"You do?"

"Good, bad, and ugly. I'm invested in you, Coral," he'd said. "I want to know everything about you. And your great-grandmother is a part of it."

I waited there as he came around the car toward me.

"I hate to make you sit back there," he whispered in my ear, and gave me a sweet kiss on the lips. He'd cleaned up nicely and brought with him the scent of sandalwood. "Grandma asleep?"

I nodded. The trip to my dad's restaurant had worn her out. "You wouldn't believe what a good time she had."

He tweaked my chin as he headed up Aunt Allie's steps. "We'll walk the beach this evening," he promised.

The door creaked open, and Aunt Allie stepped out in her church shoes. She carried a lace handkerchief and patent leather purse. She paused at the top of the steps and motioned toward the vehicle with her hankie. "Did I hear this was once Rosella's car?" she asked. Then she paused for a beat. "My, oh, my. I'm just trying to picture her in there behind the wheel, and I'm not sure I can."

Matt and I laughed.

Then, with him at her elbow, she descended the steps. Once we had her situated, she expressed her amazement at Rosella's moxie for driving such a *fancy sports car*.

Matt grinned as he started the engine and headed east down the main coastal road, Highway 98.

The term *highway* makes 98 sound large, but it's only a two-lane road. Along its south side, between the pines and palmettos, stretch long glimpses of the sparkling blue waters of the Gulf of Mexico. The road is only a few feet above sea level, and I shuddered to imagine how high and dangerous the waves might rise in a storm.

We cruised through Lanark, Panacea, Crawfordville, St. James, and Sopchoppy while Grandma told of ancient pirates, the area's salt-making during the Civil War, and the railroad my great-grandfather had worked for. In 1948 when the railroad to Carrabelle closed, my great-grandfather's work took him north to Tallahassee. Even so, he and Allie refused to give up the store that his father, my great-great-grandfather, had built back in 1889.

Matt eventually turned us around so we headed west. We would soon be back at the store. Her stories were all fascinating, and I should have been taking notes. And though I wanted to learn more about my great-grandparents, I yearned to hear something more about her daughter, Allie's one and only child—my grandmother.

So I asked.

"Althea. Althea was her name," Allie said, her voice sad. I couldn't see her face. "I named her after the most beautiful flower in my yard. The purple althea. Such a lovely baby. I was thirty-nine."

Matt turned and gave her a sympathetic look.

I kept quiet and let her talk.

"I had a dream," she said. "I knew. I just knew when she was gone. And I knew it was Horace that did it. He was so evil to her. We wanted to help her, but we didn't even know where to find her."

I reached forward and touched her shoulder.

"I pray to God that some of the things I taught her stuck," she said. As we pulled up next to the store again, she placed her own hand on mine and turned a bit in my direction. "But I think they did. She had a rough time of it. But in the end, I'm pretty sure they stuck."

I didn't want to bring up tragic things, but I so longed for more. And I hoped she'd come through for me.

8

Sol leaned back against the Greyhound bus's seat. The last rays of setting sun colored his arm and chest. After twelve hours in this uncomfortable buggy, his back side was screaming, and his shirt, a favorite Hawaiian one, was now wrinkled and stale. He hated being stale. If only these buses had a shower. He leaned forward to the driver. "Say, buddy, what time you think this bus'll pull into the parking lot in Tallahassee?" He couldn't remember how long this trip from Ft. Myers was supposed to take.
Either the driver didn't hear him, or he was ignoring him.

"Say, buddy, 'dja hear my question? What time does this crate get to Tallahassee?"

The driver held up four fingers.

"Four? Four more hours?" Sol wanted to know. The driver never answered. "Aw, never mind," he said, giving up.

He reached in his wallet and pulled out his mother's address in Carrabelle, Florida. Only then did he realize it said *Bentley's Store.* "What the heck? A store?" He stuffed the paper back in his wallet and leaned against the headrest.

No telling how long his drive from Tallahassee to Carrabelle would take. He'd have to check the book of maps that Term gave him back in Ft. Myers. But it was packed away up top in the luggage rack.

A sadness enveloped Sol as he thought back to Term and what a good buddy he'd been. Funny, Term being the hitchhiker, was always there when Sol needed him. Almost supernatural if you believed in all that. Their trip from California to Ft. Myers had been—well, different.

And then for Term to just say good-bye and walk away like he had… Sol could still feel the lump in his chest. Like a dry sandwich that wouldn't go down.

He'd never had a friend like Term.

Never had a friend, period.

And considering the odds, Sol would probably never see him again.

Sol glanced through the window at the colorless landscape. The sun hung low behind black trees. He closed his eyes. Two seconds later, he opened them again. Shoot. How could he relax?

First off, if the driver was right about arriving in four hours, it would be close to midnight when they reached the city. Stores would be closed.

He crossed his arms and shifted in the seat, trying to get comfortable, and then tried closing his eyes again. But a miserable hamster wheel turned round and round in his head as he tried to figure out where he'd sleep or if the driver would even wake him up if he fell asleep and if he'd end up in Atlanta or somewhere up the coast and his mom could even be dead by the time he got to Carrabelle.

Sol needn't worry about the driver waking him up. There he stood, in front of Sol's face. "Sir, sir, this is your stop in Tallahassee. Time to get off."

Sol shook himself awake, rubbed his eyes, and then staggered to his feet. His hips and legs, stiff from all the sitting, seemed to feel their age. He turned around to look, and the rest of the seats in the bus were completely empty. Either he was last, or the bus had emptied out while he slept.

As he reached for his bag in the compartment overhead, it slid out and fell neatly into his hands.

He couldn't wait to clean up and change, and the handiest place would be a restroom inside the bus station.

The man at the desk looked up as he entered the station. "The station will be closing at 11:59, sir."

"Thank you," Sol said, as he stretched and eyed the layout of the place. He spotted the black and white men's room icon and headed straight for it. He shoved open its door. "Well, I guess I won't be sleeping here in the station," he mumbled as he parked in front of the mirror. He reached for the soap to lather up as he studied his beard. It was now an ugly stubble. But his soap-dispenser hand came up empty. "Are you kidding?" He turned and banged the dispenser. Nothing. "Rats." He tried the paper towels. Not one.

So, he settled for plain water and the tail of his shirt and stepped back through the lobby and out into the night with his bag.

He stood there under the station's naked light bulb and wondered which direction he should go to find a hotel. Maybe he should go back inside and ask the guy at the desk.

But as he turned toward the door his vision went black.

$$9$$

Down at Bentley's store, Ralph sat on the old orange crate beside Allie in her rocking chair. His head hung low, and his elbows rested against his knees. In front of them sat the Franklin stove with its scent of cold ashes. His humble seat, its wood a hundred years old, remained constant throughout the years as they talked of his schoolwork, projects, biblical things, and even his mama dying. And sitting here today made him feel like a kid again—a guilty one.

Aunt Allie held still—she'd always been his rock of wisdom—as he let it all out.

He'd dropped the ball. Failed her, failed himself, his father, and most of all Nadine.

Ralph had crashed and burned. Then run away—to the Army, of all places. He huffed at the stupidity of running to make things better.

And then—all those wasted years avoiding her—and now, twenty years after the fact, he still had to face her.

He closed his wet eyelashes and inhaled.

Crossing the bridge earlier, his knees had trembled and threatened to give way as he headed to the store to face the music. Finally, finally—he'd forced himself to come, to get his carcass on down here and get this talk over with—and to confess to Aunt Allie about Nadine. Face to face.

Only he still couldn't look her in the eyes. He wiped the back of his hand across his cheek. Twenty years had not erased his shame.

She patted his back and gave it a rub, her hand frail against his broad shoulders. Told him once again it was okay.

"How can you even forgive me?" he whispered.

"She came to you. Didn't you try to help her, son?"

Yes, he'd hidden Nadine. Hidden her from certain death. Up to this moment he'd been careful to hold back on some of the facts, lest he crush Aunt Allie with them—the truth of what Nadine's father did to her. It was Horace Smith's baby Nadine lost back in the woods with no doctor's care. Her father's child, not Ralph's.

He gave her the slightest nod.

"You did try."

He sighed.

"And you saved her life?" Allie knew about Horace's gun. He'd busted into her place too. A guilty man who knew his jig was up. With his daughter Nadine free to speak in society, he'd surely pay for his sin. In Ralph's mind, there was no question what the man would do to Nadine if he found her. He'd take her back in the woods and kill her.

Nadine's mother had discovered it and paid with her own life. Nadine had not witnessed the killing, but when her mother disappeared after confronting him, she was sure of it.

Aunt Allie patted Ralph's back. "I'm sure you saved Nadine's life." She turned his face toward her. "And for that I truly thank you."

Poor girl. Ralph had kept her upstairs for months. Like a canary that couldn't leave its cage.

Aunt Allie's hand returned to his shoulder. "I'm not condoning everything you did. But Nadine was a beautiful girl, wasn't she? And yes, what you did later—that was wrong."

Ralph grimaced, his gaze unfocused on the wood floor. He nodded.

"And you've repented over and over, I'll bet."

His tears welled up, dropped onto the dusty wood planks between his feet. He wiped his nose on his sleeve. "She'd cry herself to sleep," he said. "Her father was the devil."

"I gathered that the few times he brought Nadine and her mother to town. As if they were on a leash. They'd get maybe five minutes in here with me, you know, while he left and did his business. Then he'd be back to snatch them away."

Ralph shook his head. "Pure evil."

Aunt Allie leaned back, and he finally straightened. His loss wasn't the only one. For the first time he looked her in the eyes.

She shook her head. "Horace Smith was probably a made-up name. My husband and I never found him."

"Smith. That's original."

"Things were different back then. People could really hide."

Ralph kept his thoughts to himself. He needed to go find that campsite.

Aunt Allie tightened her lips and blinked behind her glasses as if holding back. Then she glanced down to reach for his hand. "You must forgive yourself, son. I've had to do the same thing. You don't think we wanted to find her? My husband George would have certainly found some justice if we had."

Ralph gripped her hand and let out a long shaky breath.

"Ask God to take your mistakes—nothing is hidden from Him. And we're all full of mistakes, full of sin—ask Him to turn it around and use it for His good."

Ralph shook his head. He was so full of rot.

"The Bible tells us all our righteousness is as filthy rags," she said.

Ralph studied her face.

"I mean that. We don't measure up. But we make our best effort to do right."

"I…"

"You've long ago asked Him to forgive you. Now sit there and let the blood that Jesus shed cleanse you and make you new."

Ralph wrapped an arm around her, buried his head against her shoulder, and wept, his shoulders heaving. "I'm so sorry…"

"Son, son." She patted his head.

After a bit he sat up, "Excuse me," he said, and wiped his nose on his shirt again.

"Your Heavenly Father always forgives the humble and contrite heart. And I forgave you long ago."

He breathed through his mouth as he dried his cheeks on his sleeves.

"Now go walk a straight line."

"I will," he whispered and began to stand. But she tugged him back by the sleeve.

"None of us are worthy. None. Or we'd all go to hell. Why do you think we need to be so thankful that Jesus died on that cross?"

He nodded and stood. Then he leaned down and gave her a kiss on top of her white hair. "I love you, Aunt Allie. Thank you."

As he strode to the door, he breathed easy—as if a heavy weight had lifted away.

Ralph returned from Aunt Allie's in a lighter mood. Cleansed. Hopefully, the restaurant hadn't gone to pot while he was away. But as he stepped into the dining room from out in the brilliant sunshine, and his eyes adjusted, he could tell he'd picked a bad time to leave. Tables were jam-packed.

Larry was up front taking an order. Millie was taking orders in the back, and Jack the dishwasher appeared to be running the fryer.

Good golly. Ralph had only been gone a few minutes.

The door opened behind him, another customer. A girl. He approached. "How many?" he asked.

She smacked her gum and tilted her head under its turquoise-blue wig. Or was it her hair? He'd never seen such colorful stuff. And black lipstick?

"Just one," she said, and pointed to herself with her black fingernail. "But I've already talked to Larry, over there." She caught Larry's eye and blew him a kiss. "He said I should come back when Ralph the boss arrived. I guess that's you?"

Ralph frowned. "So—how can I help you?"

"Your sign says you need a waitress?" She struck a pose, jammed a hand on her hip, and smiled. "The name's Delia, and here I am."

Whoa. This was not what Ralph had in mind.

Well, her New Jersey accent sure stood out. But maybe a hire like this would liven up the place. Ralph's instincts screamed, *No way!* But he beat them down. He'd given his word. Justification raced through his mind like cars around a speedway. Ralph was a man of his word Then, first and foremost was the promise to Millie that he'd hire the first applicant.

A new waitress would help Millie. She was working too hard. His guy Larry needed to be in the kitchen, not out on the floor.

And now Ralph was in desperate need of some time with Coral, and… Ralph blew out a breath. The excuses had gained ground. "I'll get you some paperwork," he said. "But first, have you had waitress experience?"

She winked. "Experience is my middle name."

"Wait here," he said, pivoting quickly away from the blue eyes and extreme eyeliner.

When he returned, Delia took the paper between two fingers and laid it on the register table to fill out quickly. "You'll want me back at what time…?" she asked, handing it back.

He gave her a time for in the morning.

"Say, are there any apartments in this town? A place I could unpack my bags and kick off my shoes?"

He remembered the last time he offered one of Millie's cabins and got into big trouble with her. He wasn't about to do that again. "Hold on a minute."

He stepped over to Millie as she approached the kitchen window and whispered his request.

Millie turned slightly and out of the corner of her eye looked the girl up and down. "What in the heck is going on?" she asked between gritted teeth. "Don't tell me you hired—*that*. This is a family restaurant."

Ralph swallowed. Millie hadn't even spoken to the girl, and she had her hackles up.

He reasoned with Millie, reciting his excuses. "I did promise you. I can't renege on my word, can I?"

"Listen Ralph. All I've got is Cabin Three, half-hidden by a fallen tree and jammed tight with extra furniture." She pointed at the ceiling. "Stuff that will have to be hauled upstairs here at the restaurant. And how would that work with no elevator?"

"Could you leave it all in the cabin? Give her a discount for crowded conditions?"

Millie jammed her knuckles against her hips and blew a breath. "I don't even want to rent to her, and now you want me to give her a discount?"

"Please, Millie, I'm doing this because you need the help."

She pointed at Ralph. "I'm not moving furniture. And I want a month in advance. In the meantime, she needs to be looking around for something else to rent." She motioned with her chin toward the girl. "And those short skirts have gotta go."

Ralph shook his head and lifted his palms. "That's something you'll have to tell her, honey. I can't. And I'm puttin' you in charge of her."

"And I don't want her anywhere near Larry or Jack the dishwasher."

He turned. "Okay, okay, honey. Have at it. You're in charge."

10

I took my coffee mug out to the porch rocking chair and settled in while I waited on Aunt Allie, aka Grandma Allie, who was finishing up her breakfast with Grandma Rosella—two close buddies these days. Jessica was upstairs getting ready for work. Jessica is Grandma Rosella's home-health nurse with a flexible schedule. She met Grandma Allie about the same time we did, and we all ended up boarding here at the same time. We all love her, and she's the closest thing to a sister I ever had.

The grandmas' sewing projects had evolved into quilt designs, and even I was getting interested. I sort of hated to bust up their morning routine to take Grandma Allie away.

"Ya'll go on," Grandma Rosella said. "I can't fit into the back of that Mustang. Anyway, I'll enjoy some nice quiet time. And who knows? I might even step over and annoy Matt while he's working on Millie's tree."

Matt would love that. He wouldn't be going out on the boat today, because Zeke was out of town on business.

The screen door squeaked open, and out came Jessica.

She looped her ID badge around her neck. "Hey, Coral, Aunt Allie says you're taking her up to Apalachicola this morning. Wish I could go."

"I wish you could, too," I said. "She grew up there, so I hope she'll fill me in on some old family history."

Jessica, authentic and caring, had evolved into the sister I never had. She straightened her scrubs. "Maybe next time."

"Of course. Anytime."

"I'm so glad you've found your dad, and your great-grandmother.

Super double blessing. I keep trying to get my mom to tell me who my dad is."

"Wish you weren't working such long hours. We'd have a chance to talk." Her flexible hours had been catching up with her.

"I'll get it evened out soon," she said. "But listen, if you're any-where near Buckles Book Store around lunchtime today, stop on by. I'll be inside."

"Yeah?"

"I'm looking for a cookbook. Any kind of cookbook. Aunt Allie knows all her recipes by heart, and I hate to keep asking her how to do everything."

I laughed. Jessica wasn't used to cooking from scratch.

I set my coffee on the arm of the chair. "About what you said, Jessica, I think your mom will eventually tell you. Just give it time and keep asking."

She descended the steps. "Better get going. I've got a bunch of patients to see today." Jessica was a traveling nurse for people like Grandma Rosella. In fact, that's how we met when we first came up here. When our stay extended, making the bed-and-breakfast too expensive, and Jessica moved out of her apartment, we all ended up renting from Aunt Allie about the same time. Like it was meant to be. "See you later, I hope."

I waved. "Be safe."

She started around to the front of the building where her car was parked, and I stopped her. "Hey, why don't you come along when Dad takes me out to see Mama's old home place?"

Jessica waved back. "Wouldn't miss it!"

"Might be soon," I said, and she disappeared around the corner.

Aunt Allie and I had solved the name conundrum by the time we crossed the bridge.

"What should I call you?" I wanted to know. In my mind, I'd been trying different names.

"Call me anything you like," she said.

"Okay, then, it's Grandma Allie," I said, slowing the Mustang. I'd borrowed it from Matt this morning. "But do you mind? I need to stop by the restaurant and see Dad a minute." The term Daddy now sounded too childish to me. "Then we'll get on down the road to Apalachicola. Would you like to get out a minute?" I only needed a few words with him.

"Ralph and I have accomplished our long-overdue chit-chat, so I'll agree to eat lunch with you there sometime," she said, "but these knees, you know… I'll sit this one out in the car."

I parked with the sun behind us, opened the windows, and headed inside. Dad spotted me before my eyes even adjusted. He met me by the register.

"Coral, what brings you in so early today? What can I get you?"

I explained our mission of the day. "But," I said, "have you given my request any thought?"

"Given it thought?" He was playing dumb, and I shook my head. I'd seen this ploy before with people who didn't want to say no to your face.

Busted, his laughter filled the room.

I crossed my arms in mock irritation. "You know what I'm talking about. I need to learn about my family. The same reason I'm taking Grandma Allie up the coast this morning."

"Aw, honey," he hedged. "I've been completely swamped. But give me a little time. You may not like what you're gonna learn."

Before he could talk me out of anything, I turned and waved good-bye. "Gotta go now. Thank you!"

It certainly couldn't hurt to go out and see the place.

11

Beeping monitors and a pounding headache stirred Sol. He cracked open his eyelids. The sight around him widened them further. Under and over him stretched clean white sheets. A clock and markerboard hung on the wall past his feet.

What is this, a dang hospital?

He eased himself up, pausing halfway as the throbs broadened and then diminished. *Better take it slow*, he figured and reached for the bedrail. This movement disturbed the IV line taped to the back of his hand and its bag next to his bed. He scowled and pulled himself upright, resenting the idea of being tethered by a dang needle under that tape. He reached around with his other hand to explore the gauze around his head and decided to leave it alone.

"Nurse!" he tried to yell but winced as a fresh stab ricocheted through his skull.

In the meantime, a nurse raced into the room followed by another. "Our mystery man's awake," the first one said. She touched his shoulder. "Sir, please lie down. You shouldn't be getting excited."

"I figured that out," he mouthed and eased back down. "What happened?"

"You were hit in the back of the head, a pretty hard blow. But the good news is, it didn't break your skull. And your brain isn't bleeding."

He grimaced. "Got an aspirin?"

The nurse smiled. "We'll get you something. Do you have any allergies?"

Sol shrugged. He had no idea.

The first nurse left, and the second came back in with a

policeman. "He's here to ask you a few questions," she said. "Do you feel up to it?"

"No, not really," Sol whispered as the first nurse returned and fiddled with the bag. She administered something through his IV.

The policeman proceeded anyway. "Last night an employee at the Greyhound bus station found you unconscious out on the front porch of the station. It looks like you had a blow to the back of the head. When we arrived, you had no ID."

"Check my wallet," Sol mumbled.

"Sir, you were robbed. You have no wallet."

Sol's eyes drifted shut.

The officer continued, "Could you give us your name and tell us what happened?"

Sol lay still. *Give us your name and tell us…* He would have to think about that. Think about that… Then sleep enveloped him like a warm blanket.

Hours later, when Sol opened his eyes, he tried sitting up. His brain still throbbed. The monitor behind him continued its beeps. But this time the IV's flow was clamped off. As he turned toward the paper and pen on the bedside table, he caught sight of a nurse passing by his door.

"Nurse," he called out. What the heck? His voice sounded old and feeble, not like his own. "Nurse."

But she hadn't heard him.

He braced himself and yelled. "Nurse!"

This drew her back to the door. "Oh, my, you're looking better," she said, and came on in. "How do you feel?"

He closed his eyes and lifted his fingers. How'd she think he felt? "You got any food?"

The nurse smiled. "I'm glad you're feeling better. We'll get you something to eat."

She stepped around his bed and pulled the bedside table up close. "Do you remember the policeman coming up and talking to you? He'll be back, but he wanted your name and address."

"He said I got robbed." Sol fingered his hospital gown. "Did they take my bag?"

She walked over to the closet and pulled out his travel bag. "The policeman put your things back in. It seems the robbers went through it. The good news is the bad guys left your clothes and personal items. And this book." She pulled out Term's Atlas, the one he'd given Sol. And Sol was glad to see it. "But the police found no wallet or phone. Now that you're awake, I'm supposed to call the officer back. Think you can handle a talk with him?"

"As long as you don't put me to sleep again. What about the clothes I had on?"

She returned to the closet, lifted out a white plastic bag, and laid it on the bed. "They're all in here."

He pulled open the bag and looked in. On top were his shorts, underwear, and flip flops. Beneath them he found his shirt, stiff now, with disgusting brown stains. "Naww," he whined. "Not my favorite Hawaiian shirt."

"Head wounds do bleed a lot. But you might not have to throw it away," the nurse offered. "They have products…"

He stuffed it back in the bag.

"Yeah," had said, relieved that it wasn't the one Paulette had given him. At least he had a change of clothes. He eyed the Atlas again as he opened the other bag and crammed the bag with dirty clothes inside. A shirt he could replace, but not that Atlas. His friend Term had even written a note in it. His only friend.

He had to get out of this place and go get Eddie's car out of that paint shop. But how was he going to do that without a wallet?

His stomach was screaming, but the nurse left with the promise of food "The supper cart is coming soon," she said.

He sank down in the bed, exhausted. Supper? He stared at the clock on the wall. Had he slept all day? The paint shop would be closing. And without the car he'd have no place to stay. Again.

Sol grimaced as a blast of pain exploded through his head. If he asked for more pain meds, they'd knock him out again. So he decided to tough it out.

Decision time. Ready or not, tomorrow after breakfast—and a

shower—he'd walk out of here. He twisted around to locate the bathroom door, a thing he hadn't even bothered with.

Come to think of it, two days here and he hadn't used a bathroom? He lifted the cotton blanket and checked himself. *Shoot.*

He'd also have to wait until they took the stupid catheter out.

Matt glanced down at his phone and checked for missed calls. Dad never texted, but he'd certainly call—with at least one gripe or complaint—might be bad traffic, bad gas mileage, or some bozo driving like a maniac. But so far no missed calls. Dad must be having a pretty good trip.

12

The next morning after breakfast, Sol raised a fuss until the nurse removed his catheter. He couldn't afford not to. After she left, he yanked the bandage off the back of his hand, gritted his teeth, and pulled out the needle. He dumped this mess on the bedside table, made use of the facilities, and cleaned up good. Then, wearing a change of clothes, he slipped down the hall and into the elevator. And there, on wobbly knees, and grateful the thing was empty, he leaned against the wall to get the shakes out. He wanted nothing more than to sit down and wondered the whole ride down why elevators didn't have any dang benches in them, for goodness' sake.

At ground level, the door slid open, and down the hall he pattered, straight through the front door in his clean bermudas and flip flops. Not a soul stopped him.

Outside on the sidewalk he slowed to a crawl and located a bench near the hospital's front fountain to collapse for a spell. If they were going to hunt him down, this would be a good place. But not a single person spoke or even bothered him. It took a lot of will power, but after a time, as wonderful as the repose was, he forced himself to stand and move on. Crossing through the parking lot, he asked a random couple for directions and then found his way to the the auto paint shop and its customer service desk. No chairs here, either. He leaned against the desk. Thank goodness the paint shop was near the hospital.

But a lot of good it did him.

"I'm sorry, Mr. Flores, we realize your vehicle's paint job is complete," the teen employee said, "but I can't release the car to you without an ID."

Sol slammed his fist on the counter. "I was..." He paused as a painful throb reminded him to lower his voice. "I was just here a few days ago." He pointed to his face, "Look at this mug. It's me, Sol Flores. And now you need ID? How many people you got goin' through here with a new paint job and a sparkly racing stripe going down the side? Huh? Huh? Just tell me that."

"I'm sorry, sir, that's just our policy. You have to have your ID."

"Now, ain't that just dandy. First I get mugged, and now the paint shop's stealin' my car."

Sol leaned across the counter and considered his options. "Look, if I can get you some other photo ID in my name, somethin' else besides a driver's license, will that do?" He had no idea what that would be, though.

The young twit, probably brand new at the job, turned around and signaled to the mirror behind him. Only then did Sol realize it was a two-way.

The boy stepped to the side, and Sol caught a look at his own reflection. At that point he realized how stupid he'd just sounded. With his bandaged head and two black eyes, not to mention that fast growing stubble, he looked like somebody else. In his haste this morning to snag that free breakfast and shower before fleeing the hospital's clutches, he'd skipped the shave.

As he gazed at his reflection, a clean-cut man, probably the manager, stepped around the mirrored wall and approached the register. At the same time, Sol grabbed the edge of the counter as a dizzy spell hit—a thing the nurse warned might happen. The room spun, and the man's image doubled—tripled if one counted the mirror. Sol closed his eyes and waited for the feeling to pass.

"Yes sir," the man said. "We'll be glad to take another form of ID. And we're sorry this happened to you. Can you get somebody to fax it to us?"

Sol slowly reopened his eyes and aimed his hand toward one of the doubles. "I appreciate that, sir. You the owner?"

But to Sol's chagrin, the other figure took his hand.

The man studied Sol's bandage and smiled. "I'm sorry you got mugged, sir, and I know that head's gotta hurt. Come on to the back and sit down in my office where we can talk it over and come up with a plan." He turned and walked back through his doorway.

Sol was only too glad to cooperate.

But as he stepped forward he had to grab the counter again as a new wave of vertigo sent him spinning. He clamped his eyes shut and held on tight. The young twit stood to the side watching. Even if Sol got his car back this minute, how was he going to drive it like this?

The dizzy spell subsided, and he passed on through the doorway to find the man already seated behind his large desk to the right. Paint ads and posters of shiny cars, antique and modern, lined three walls. The glass wall facing the cash register covered the other.

"Take a seat," the man said and pointed to a plastic-covered seat. He handed Sol a cold bottle of water. "Are you okay?" he asked.

"I'll get through it," Sol answered, lowering himself carefully hoping he did get through it soon. He reduced his voice to a whisper to keep the throbs under control. "Look, if you let me use your phone—they stole mine—I'll call my shop out in Las Vegas. They can come up with something."

The man turned his desk phone toward Sol. "Take all the time you need."

Sol took the phone as the man busied himself with a stack of paperwork and his calculator.

Sol dialed, but he got nowhere. His shop number in Las Vegas rang and rang. And then he remembered. "I hate to break it to you, mister. Las Vegas is three hours behind us. And my shop opens at ten."

The clock on the paint shop's wall said ten o'clock. They'd have a three hour wait.

"That's a long time," the man said. "Would you like to lie down? It's no trouble. I'll fix you up with some coffee and more chairs to lie across."

Sol stared at the man. His head dropped, and he stared at the floor. "I would. I really would. I'm so tired. And I'm sorry I was nasty."

Sol eventually reached Eddie who contacted Paulette. She would wire him money via a Western Union hub at a nearby grocery store, plus some extra for expenses.

The generous paint shop owner gifted Sol ten dollars for lunch and dropped him off when he took his own lunch break. Once the money came through, Sol would have to walk the four blocks back to the paint shop.

Sol had another long wait on the bench in front of the store as the money worked its way through the system and landed at the customer service desk. The whole day was gone.

Sol made it back to the paint shop by late afternoon, just as the shop was closing, to seal the deal. Only then did Sol think to examine the finished paint job.

"This is good work," Sol said, admiring the vehicle. *New tires, new paint, what more could Eddie want?* Sol was pleased with himself as well as the paint shop manager.

"The sparkly racing strip was a good choice," the man told him. "Maroon paint, black sparkle along here. Classy. You have good taste."

"Paulette and Eddie came up with that stripe color," he said. Not that the man knew who they were.

As Sol threw his bag into the car and prepared to drive away, he considered how the days had flown. This time two days ago he was sitting on a bus.

"I want to thank you for all you did to help me, today, mister…"

"Rodriguez. Hector Rodriguez," the man said as they shook hands. "You sure you don't need to get a room somewhere before you take off on your trip? Could I get you some more acetaminophen before you go?"

"No," Sol said. "I don't wanna get there too late. My mama's sick—and may be dyin'.""

"Aw, I'm sorry. I'll be praying for you, man. For your safety. For your mama."

"Thank you, Hector." And Sol really meant it. He hoped Hector wouldn't forget those prayers.

By early evening, Ralph glanced up from the fryer to the side door. Zeke and Matt would be knockin' on that thing any minute. And in they would drag, wet and tired from today's charter and the clean-up of Zeke's beautiful boat, the *Gulf Princess*, and lug in the shark Zeke had called him about.

Ralph lifted the basket of fries to drain and glanced back at Larry who was mixing a salad. "Got a shark comin' in, buddy. Any second." Larry, though merely a teen, showed promise here at the restaurant—but only as long as he didn't start back to mistreating Ralph's kitties out back.

The kid, already an expert at processing shark meat and preparing their steaks, was quickly evolving into Ralph's right-hand asset.

Ralph had never mentioned to Larry about his past. "You know, Zeke and I—as kids—you couldn't tear us apart—we had big plans to do that charter boat thing—together."

"Yeah? So how'd you end up with a restaurant?"

Hmmph. The fifty-dollar question. Ralph gazed down at the plate and dumped on the fries. He'd kept that whole Nadine story a secret from Zeke. Back then, ashamed, he'd run off to the Army. Of course, his friend had to be hurt, wondering all the while what he'd done to offend Ralph. But Ralph just kept his mouth shut. Acted like nothing was up. He shifted the fries and shook his head at his own stupidity.

Ralph blinked at Larry. "My dad died."

"Sorry, Mr. Ralph. I didn't mean to—"

"No, no." Ralph waved him off and checked another order at the window. He dumped in a new batch of fries.

He glanced back at Larry. "Water over the dam or under the bridge, however they phrase it."

Ralph pressed his lips together as the oil sizzled. Poor Zeke. For the next twenty years, Ralph avoided any meaningful conversation with him—until recently when his old friend ended up saving his life. And Ralph had let it all out—every bit of it.

Zeke, like the true friend he always had been, was there for him.

Larry loaded up three salad plates. "I guess that's why Zeke brings by those sharks, huh? Feels bad for ya."

Ralph's nod seemed to satisfy Larry's curiosity.

Zeke's forgiving nature was his trademark. It never diminished over the years. Bringing sharks was just his way of saying he was there for Ralph.

A text vibrated his phone, and he glanced at the screen.

"That them?" Larry asked.

"Yep. 'Five minutes,' it says, and 'two shrimps.' You want one too, Larry?"

Larry grinned and nodded.

"I'll getcha one for your mama too." Ralph didn't mind a bit. A single mom, she wasn't in good shape these days, and Larry's support was all she had.

"Thank you, sir!"

Kid would've done just fine in the Army.

Ralph stepped to the freezer and reached for the frozen shrimp bag. He stopped midway and pointed straight at Larry. "Lemme tell you this. A friend like Zeke is hard to find. No matter why our dream fell apart—and disappointed as he might have been—not once did Zeke carry a grudge or let our friendship falter."

That's more than Ralph could say for himself.

He carried the shrimp back to the fryer, poured some in, and watched them sizzle. He was glad to prepare this treat for his friend. Zeke's charter-fishing clients weren't particularly fond of sharks, and intimidated by the size and special prep they required, usually relinquished them to the captain. So Zeke dropped them off at the restaurant for Ralph. His restaurant-goers were delighted with the occasional shark steak on the menu. And with sharks plenteous this season, the extra cash added up. Zeke wanted nothing in return but hot shrimp dinners—for him and his helper Matt. And Ralph always threw some in for Larry and his mama.

Larry was proud to be called an expert shark-chef along with his other accumulating skills.

If Ralph played things right, heck, he might actually be able to leave Larry in charge one day and spend time on the boat with Zeke. In the meantime, he kept an eye on the side door. He had a favor to ask of Matt.

14

Sol waved good-bye as he pulled away from the paint shop. Hector, in front of his now-lowered garage door, waved back. "Take care," the man said as Sol tossed in his Atlas and hid the extra cash Paulette sent him under the driver's side floor mat.

Hector didn't need to tell Sol to take care. Sol always took care. Like right now, as he noted the road number he was on and pulled over on the right to study the Atlas. He ran his finger over the lines. "South on Highway…got it." He turned onto the road again and searched for the numbered sign. "There it is," he said, easing into the left turn lane. According to the map, Carrabelle wasn't all that far. He'd be down there before he knew it.

Fifteen minutes later, Sol found himself in the middle of nowhere on a desolate road surrounded by forests of tall pines, spiky palmettos, and rain-filled swales. Not a house or a store could be seen. And very few cars.

The sun was dropping fast now. Alternating stripes of orange sun and dark shadows cut left across the asphalt. The loud buzzing of the woods surrounded him. Sol was in the middle of nowhere.

Then, with no warning, his engine lost power. It was all Sol could do to maneuver his tires onto the weedy shoulder and hope he didn't flip over into the swale. The engine was silent. Dead as dead could be.

He threw it into park and slumped in his seat, his head low. New tires, new paint, and a dead engine. This couldn't be happening.

A realization struck, and his eyes dropped to the dash. He slammed his palm against the steering wheel and glared at the panel. "I knew it!" he yelled. *E…for empty.* "Not again!" A stab of pain shot through his head, and he grabbed his forehead. He should have let Hector give him that pain reliever.

15

A loud banging rattled the kitchen's side door at The Captain's Table. Across the room, Ralph jiggled the fryer basket. "Larry!" he yelled. "Get the door!" Most certainly, it was the guys with their shark. Only Matt and Zeke ever used that door. Larry flung it wide and stepped back, flooding the kitchen with colorful rays of sunset. He gave the grunting men wide berth as they lugged in their tarp with its two-hundred-pound load of ice-covered shark.

The smell of sweat, sunshine, and fish followed them in but quickly dissipated into the overarching smell of fried seafood. They heaved the carcass up on the metal table, its cavity already emptied of guts, long-since dumped into the ocean as chum.

Larry watched in awe as they flipped it handily off the tarp. He would be responsible for processing the meat which would appear on tomorrow's menu.

Ralph gave the creature a quick glance and a nod of approval. "A good seven feet," he said and stepped back to check his fryer.

Matt and Zeke nodded, their job complete, and disappeared into the break room where they plopped down on opposite ends of the old, frayed sofa to mop their brows and rest their legs. They—and Ralph—preferred to keep their distance from the cleaner clientele.

"Hot food comin' right up," Ralph said.

In short order, he slid two steaming platters onto the battered Formica table in front of them, a table that used to belong to Ralph's mom and dad, one he'd never part with. The men bowed their heads, said their blessings, and dug in.

Zeke, with a family waiting at his house, bolted his food and headed out the back door for home. Soon after, Matt rose to tidy up the table. But Ralph stopped him. "Hang on a minute," he said and closed the door. Larry didn't need to hear all his business.

Matt settled back down. "Sure, what's up?"

Ralph took a seat. "Somethin' I think will interest you."

"Go ahead."

"I'd like you to do a little research for me. A little pokin' around and askin' questions."

"Might could. What about and who with?"

Ralph chuckled. "Listen to you—*might could*. You're soundin' more 'n more like one of us all the time."

Matt grinned. "I am one of you—now."

Ralph charged on. "Look, Coral is asking questions about her grandfather—you know, Nadine's father. Wants to go visit the old place. She's not gonna let it go until I take her."

Matt nodded. "Yeah. She mentioned it."

"Man's name is—or was—Horace Smith," Ralph said, forming air quotes around the name.

Matt frowned.

"Well, for starters, we can't let Coral know her grandfather was an incestuous devil."

Matt leaned away, as if disgusted. He shook his head.

"Sorry to dump that on you. But I think we can agree on things, Matt. If we let on about what Horace was, it could crush Coral. Or Aunt Allie. We can't tell them that."

Matt took a deep breath. "Gosh, man. Sick."

"Go ask questions. Talk to Aunt Allie. See what other info you can pick up about the creep before we go out there."

Matt, still distracted by the news continued to shake his head

Ralph cuffed his arm. "Listen, you hear what I'm tellin' you? Before *we* go out there," he pointed at Matt, then himself, "you and I, we're gonna learn what we can."

Matt finally gave him a thumbs up.

It was up to Matt to figure out how to broach the subject with Aunt Allie, but Ralph had all confidence in him.

"They lived out in Tate's Hell," Ralph said. "Squatters who didn't own property. Nadine drew out some vague directions at one time. I just hope I can remember."

"Tate's Hell? I saw that brochure. Disturbing place."

Ralph snorted. "Yeah, kinda. And a good place to hide from authorities if you have things to conceal."

Matt rubbed his chin. "According to the leaflet, it's been turned into some kind of state forest or park. Things could have changed out there, you know."

"Yeah, now, listen," Ralph raised a finger, "when we go out there, if we find evidence Aunt Allie might not oughtta hear about, like Nadine's mother's bones—Nadine swore he killed her—we'll keep it to ourselves. Or, God help us, if the old goat's still alive and kickin' back there—I've got pistols. One for you and one for me. Just so you know."

"I can shoot."

"Bottom line is, Aunt Allie's too old for a shock. And Coral—well, she's just too young and sweet for one. She don't need to know that kinda trash about her past."

Matt nodded and rose to leave. "Gotcha."

As soon as Matt gathered his info, they'd drive on out to Tate's Hell.

Matt set his toolbox on Aunt Allie's side porch and tapped on the screen door. Unlocked and loose, it rattled against the frame.

Coral, with a wadded dish towel in her hand, answered the door. "Matt!" She swung it open, and they traded a quick kiss.

"We were just finishing up," she said. "Come on in. How about some leftovers?" She pointed to the dishes on the counter behind her. Aunt Allie and Grandma Rosella, still at the table, had pretty much finished except for their dessert of biscuits and cane syrup.

"Oh, thanks, but I couldn't. Zeke and I brought in a shark, and I ate down at Ralph's—courtesy of the shark. But I'll come in."

"Sit down. Sit down," Aunt Allie said. "Biscuits and syrup?"

He patted his stomach and shook his head as he circled the table and bent to give hugs to the ladies. He took a chair while they finished up.

Grandma Rosella squeezed his hand.

After a few minutes of chit-chat, he turned to Aunt Allie. "Are you ready? I've brought over my toolbox, and I'd like to take a look at that squeaky rocking chair you've been wanting fixed. Can you come show me which one it is?"

"It's the one in the corner. All by itself."

"Okay. But can you come on out and keep me company?"

"Of course I will, Matt." She pivoted in her chair. Then with one hand on the table and her cane in the other, she stood. She shooed him out the door ahead of her. "Go on, now. I'll be right behind you."

As Matt held the door for her, he signaled to Grandma Rosella and Coral that he needed to talk to Aunt Allie and that they should stay inside.

They nodded as he followed Aunt Allie out the door.

Out on the porch he pulled up a second rocker for her.

If he was going to get more information on Horace Smith, this seemed to be the way. And it wasn't something he could do in front of Coral.

He hoped she didn't overhear.

16

Before Sol's car ran out of gas, he'd spotted very few oncoming cars on the two-lane road. And because of his conservative speed out here in the middle of nowhere, an equal number had whizzed past him—like angry hornets.

The last dim rays of orange now filtered through the woods. He imagined suppertime in homes and families winding down from their day, taking hot showers, and getting dressed for bed.

Surrounded by darkening woods he leaned out the window and surveyed the road beyond and behind. Help would never stop if he stayed in his seat behind the wheel. Sol had to do something now, right now. His maroon car would be invisible soon. Help would fly past before they knew he was there. The best thing he could do would be to stand by the car with his empty red gas can and demonstrate his predicament.

He fingered his bandage as he climbed out and slammed the door and wondered if it would help or hinder his situation.

Around back, Sol opened the trunk and considered the best spot to stand, beside the car or back here. He figured if he stood to the side, he'd end up leaning against Eddie's brand new paint job. Better to stand in the back. Then people could see him as they approached. Better than getting crushed by some edge-of-the-road driver, anyway.

With the can at his feet, he took his place behind the vehicle. And his wait turned out to be shorter than expected, a mere ten minutes.

The massive wheels of a huge Ford truck ground to a halt on the shoulder beyond him. Evidence of yard tools and mowers stuck up from its bed. The passenger door opened, and out scrambled a scrawny man in soiled work pants and a naked torso. He reached up to the side of the tilted truck bed and struggled his way up and in. He found what he was looking for and leaped out with a gas can. Judging by the way the man swung the can around, it was light and couldn't have held much liquid.

But any little bit of help right now was welcome.

At least someone stopped.

Sol waited as the guy approached. "I appreciate you stopping, sir."

"Sure thing," the man said. A rank cloud of body odor preceded him. "How you today?" His smile revealed a dark row of sawed-off teeth. The teeth reminded Sol of before and after pictures he'd seen of crack-heads—and this one seemed like the *after* version.

Sol backed away to give the man space at the gas cap and waited as he jammed the can into the opening. Sol swallowed as the man tipped it all the way up to drain its last little bit of gasoline—maybe a quart, maybe less. At the same time a wave of vertigo swept over Sol, and he grabbed the back end of the car to steady himself while it passed.

But at that same instant, the truck in front of Sol revved up and sped away.

Crack-head stayed put as if this was no big deal and he hadn't lost his ride.

"Hey!" Sol said. "Where's he going? What's happening here!" Crack-head dropped his gas can and flicked open a switchblade. He held it near Sol's neck while his mouth turned down and his beady black eyes bored into Sol's like something out of a horror movie. Sol stepped back farther.

"Yeah, you better be afraid, you weenie! Pull out your wallet."

"Th-they took it. I-I-I don't have it anymore."

The man evaluated Sol's bandage and scowled even more. "Well, ain't that just peachy," he said. "Back away! Back away."

Sol had no choice.

"Where's your phone? Where's your phone?"

"Th-they took that too."

The man put his hand on the door handle. "Don'tchu try to stop me now, or I'll run you over. Back away." He waved the knife. "Get baaack. Baaaack."

When Sol was far enough away, the man yanked open the car's door and flung himself inside, starting the engine. He stomped the gas and mud sprayed over Sol's face. The door slammed while the car took off.

Sol stood there in numb disbelief as his own car's taillights grew smaller and smaller in the twilight. The man's redneck yell rebounded through the trees, "Whoo boy! I got me a new car!"

The fading hum of Sol's engine—and the lonely sound of its tires against the pavement—disappeared into the night.

A low breeze pushed against Sol's face, and off to his right, a vein of lightning lit the distant pines. Seconds later, a roll of thunder growled.

Sol couldn't help but imagine once again the families in their cozy homes and soft pajamas.

He stood there among the crickets—and the bugs—and the croaking, buzzing forest as it grew louder around him.

17

Matt stood and turned the rocker upright. "I appreciate your filling me in on Horace, Aunt Allie." He sat and tried out the chair, giving it a few rocks. No squeaks. "And thanks for keeping me company out here. I apologize if I kept you past your bedtime." She waved him off. "Oh, *pshaw.* No bother. I enjoyed our visit."

He situated the rocker in its rightful place and packed away his tools.

The stuff he'd gathered on Coral's grandfather was a game-changer.

"Well, now that your chair is all set, I hope you have a good night. And much better dreams this time, right?" Aunt Allie had no one else she could share it with and had confided about the bad dream she'd had—the doves flying out of Grandma Rosella's fingertips. The dream gave him pause, too, but he didn't tell her. She mentioned a second nightmare but didn't share the details.

Aunt Allie nodded. "They have to be better than those."

"Give me your hand," he said, reaching over and helping her up.

After he walked her back inside, he bid Coral and Grandma Rosella a quick good night, gave each one the usual kisses and hugs, and headed toward the porch again. "I doubt I'll see you in the morning," he said as he eased the door almost shut. "It might be as late as tomorrow afternoon."

He waved good-bye, pulled it shut, and then headed off to Ralph's to fill him in.

As he arrived at the restaurant's back door, Ralph was just locking up.

"Ralph. Guess I'm just in time," Matt said.

Ralph pocketed the key and lowered himself onto the metal

steps next to the door. His apartment was two floors up. One of the back-door kittens raced over to Ralph and meowed, rubbing against his socks. Ralph picked him up and rubbed his ears to loud purrs. "Long day," he said and pointed a thumb at the step beside him. "Have a seat. I guess you're worn out, and I know I am. So just give me the five-minute version for now, and I'll catch the rest in the morning."

"I apologize, Ralph."

"No, kiddo, it's like this every night. I'm beat. But go ahead, I've been waiting for you, and I wanna hear it."

"Then I'll keep it short." Matt leaned against the rail instead of sitting and relayed the information as briefly as possible. In the meantime, the cat had had enough and leaped down, scampering away.

Matt rolled out a brief synopsis, and Ralph slapped his knees and stood. "It all makes sense, doesn't it?" Then he paused. "Since Zeke's not going out tomorrow," he said, "we'll go on up to Tate's Hell in the morning. At seven. We ought to be back by ten."

Matt leaned away from the rail. "You bet. Get some rest now." He turned away to head back across the bridge as Ralph climbed the stairs. Gravel crunched lightly beneath Matt's sneakers. The town was quiet with hardly a soul in sight. Carrabelle was a decent little early-to-bed town, the exact opposite of the never-ending nights of Las Vegas, his hometown. Matt rather appreciated it.

He turned left at Millie's cabin and followed the fallen log. Blue light glowed behind Millie's curtains, probably from her television. He imagined her in there with her feet up after a hard day.

As he fished out the key to his own quarters, Cabin Two, a female's voice startled him. "Hey, there, big boy."

He twisted to the right only to spot the red tip of a cigarette near the steps of Cabin Three. The dark night revealed nothing but a woman's silhouette against the cabin door. He decided to ignore her.

"Whatcha up to?" she said. Whoever she was, she sounded inebriated.

He dismissed the comment and shoved open his door.

"Act stuck up if you want to," she said, "but I'm your new neighbor.

Anytime you wanna come on over an' pay me a visit, now, you just slip on over and visit. You hear?"

Neighbor? What the heck? There was no way Millie could be renting out that third cabin. The thing was packed tight with furniture—big stuff she couldn't have possibly moved.

He stepped into his cabin, shut the door, and locked it.

Despite the annoyance of the new neighbor, Matt fell right to sleep.

But somewhere in the middle of the night a thought stirred him awake. A thought of Dad. He raised up on one elbow and cast a glance at the clock. Two a.m.

He reached for his phone. Had his father even tried to call?

He clicked on his comments and checked for missed calls.

Not a one.

Matt frowned. This didn't add up. He dialed Dad's number. But the phone rang and rang and then went to voicemail.

Dad wouldn't be talking this late at night. And he would certainly answer a ring.

Matt dropped the phone beside him again and sank back on his pillow, his eyes riveted on the ceiling.

After a minute, he rolled over and dropped his knees to the floor.

He'd better pray about this.

Something wasn't right.

18

Sol considered walking along the roadway to Carrabelle. But in his current state, vertigo would probably hit. He'd fall over on the asphalt and along would come some other giant truck with big tires and flatten him out like that armadillo he passed back there. He wouldn't last the night.

Besides, how many miles away was Carrabelle? He was already tired.

He'd have to find a clearing over there in the palmettos.

As he followed the edge of the pavement he concentrated on the racket of the wildlife. Like it or not, he'd have to spend the night out here with them—and hope all the panthers and the bears were busy far away.

Other people camped out, didn't they? Maybe Sol could.

He eyed the rain-filled ditches below him. Barely visible now, they reflected the last blush of sunset and would soon appear like black holes. Too wide to leap, their presence moved him along, in search of a narrow crossing.

Yards in the distance appeared a light-colored patch leading off the pavement. As he drew near, he found it to be a stone-covered culvert where someone, some time ago, had dumped a load of gravel. Whoever the man was he was long gone now. He was probably in front of his TV with a hot plate of spaghetti and garlic toast to enjoy and probably couldn't even remember this delivery out in the middle of nowhere.

Stop it, Sol told himself and gazed down into the rocks.

They led off the highway to nowhere.

Who would go to the trouble of dumping a truckload of rocks for no reason at all? It didn't make sense.

Nevertheless, Sol crossed over to the other side in search of a clearing. A clearing where he could camp for the first time ever and at least bide his time until daylight. The trees stood around him now like a black wall.

He shivered in his thin shirt as the wind picked up and stared into the darkness as another bolt of lightning, closer this time, lit it up and revealed an opening in the foliage to his right. He felt his way along as thunder followed. And there he paused, hoping for more lightning. As its frequency increased, lighting his way, he followed the breaks deeper and deeper into the scrub. The injury to his head throbbed now, and he knew this was no ideal way to spend his night. He thought back to the mud on his face and felt his bandage. He hoped his stitches didn't get infected. But then the stitches weren't in the front.

Lightning brightened the woods again, followed by near-immediate thunder. The storm was upon him. Once again, he followed its lead. He needed a clearing, something more detached from the palmettos, where he'd heard that the rattlesnakes sleep.

Sol shivered at the thought and hoped they slept at night, too.

Lightning struck again, leading him deeper along the path. Then, as rain's first heavy drops began to ping the fronds around him, he found himself in a small grassy clearing, about ten by ten. At its center rose a tall dead tree, its bark skinned naked by the forces of nature. His bedroom in the woods. As he dove for its roots, the rain let loose. It blasted sideways, soaking him through and through. Chilled and trembling, he balled up and huddled as best he could against the trunk. It shielded him to some degree from the brunt of the storm, and it gave him some small comfort to know that at least he had a spot to call home for the night.

Pulling his flip-flopped feet up tighter under his buttocks, he tried not to think of snakes and bears and panthers and bobcats. Maybe the rain would rinse away his scent or keep them holed up in a log somewhere. At least he hoped so.

19

The next morning, Matt showered. He pulled on his tee shirt and cargo pants and stepped out of his cabin to head up to Ralph's—but not before tossing a cautious glance toward Cabin Three. Its steps were now empty. Cigarette butts lay scattered in the gravel around them.

Next time he got the chance he'd have to ask Millie about the new renter. In the meantime, he pushed it aside and headed up the bridge enjoying the sunshine and the loud boisterous calls of the floating gulls.

On the other end of the bridge, The Captain's Table's parking lot seemed unusually full for so early in the morning. If Ralph wanted to go out to Tate's Hell this morning, it looked like he might have trouble getting away.

Sure enough, Millie greeted him with, "Mornin' Matt. Ralph says he's elbow deep, and it's gonna be a minute. So just go ahead and have a seat there," she said, indicating a nearby booth. "I'll get you somethin' to eat. Don't you worry, though, he won't be too long." She stepped away toward the order window. "Be right back with your coffee, honey."

As Millie turned away, a new waitress appeared out of nowhere and pivoted her hip against his table. She could have been posing for a magazine with that little order pad. She winked. "What can I get you, big man?" She crossed her arms. "You are so dang *cuute!*"

He glanced up to see a blue-haired girl of about twenty. Caught off guard, he shook his head and waved his hand as if to say no and finally found his voice. "I've already been waited on."

Millie returned with her cup and coffeepot. She gave the girl a toss of her chin and said, "Delia, these are my tables." She pointed around the corner. "You go tend to that dining room."

Delia gave her a syrupy smile and stepped away.

"I'm so sorry Matt, she isn't supposed to be over here."

"Is that…?" The girl's voice sounded familiar, like the one he heard last night.

"My new renter," she whispered, "And I'm so sorry, Matt. I'm trying to do something about it, but it just…just happened. I'll explain later."

Matt gave a low whistle. "Yeah. I'd sure like to hear that."

Millie shook her head. "You have no idea. She's like a spider. I'm trying to keep her off of Jack and Larry back there, too."

Matt shook his head. "Unbelievable."

At The Captain's Table, things slowed down just enough so Ralph could set Larry up over at the fryer. "Stay right here, and do what's needed," he told him and then headed toward the back door.

He arm-signaled Matt. "C'mon, and don't turn around, or we'll end up right back in there," he told him, plunging through the screen door and over to his parked truck. Ralph leaped into the truck before Matt, and they headed down the road toward Tate's Hell.

Once they passed the entry gate, Ralph focused on dodging holes on the dirt road as they bounced along.

Between potholes he eyed Matt briefly. "You thinkin' what I'm thinkin'?"

Before Matt could answer, he took the left fork to follow the ruts deeper into Tate's Hell. This would surely take them down to spring-fed streams that flowed into the Carrabelle River. He glanced west toward the slate blue sky and hoped they'd beat the daily storms. The race was on.

After Matt stopped by to see him last night, Ralph was more determined than ever to make this trip.

Just those short bits of information convinced Ralph they should get down there and check things out.

"So what are you thinking?" Matt said.

"Look behind the cooler back there."

Matt twisted around in his seat and peered into the backseat. He gave Ralph a quizzical look. "You brought a metal detector?"

"Everybody owns one around these parts." Ralph grinned. "Never know what you'll find at the beach."

Matt gripped the edge of the seat as Ralph's big tires conquered a rise and a sudden drop. "Wait, what beach? Thought we were headed down to the river."

Ralph laughed. "Just kiddin'. But think about it, Matt. The gold coin Coral found?"

"I heard about it, but I haven't seen it yet."

"Well, you will. But I know for sure the coin wasn't in the shell when I gave it to Nadine. It had to come from Nadine herself. Had to. So, where'd she get it?"

"Home, I guess. Unless you had coins laying around upstairs in the apartment."

"Nope." Ralph gripped the wheel with both fists. "All right, listen. If Aunt Allie's right—and Horace was, indeed, a miserly hoarder that traded all his cash for gold—then theoretically his stash could still be down at the camp. If he's moved, then he took it. But if he's dead—well, we ought to at least look around. And he very well could be dead. He was a whole lot older than his wife back then. Seventy if he was a day."

Matt switched his grip to the dash as the road gave them a workout.

Ralph tipped his thumb toward the space beneath the passenger seat. "Check under there. You're all set with a loaded pistol."

Matt gave him a slow nod.

It would be stupid to go down there unarmed. He hoped they found the camp, but they couldn't afford to be ambushed by the old geezer. "Two ways this can play out. One, if he's still out there, he'll be armed. But he hasn't shown his face for as long as I can remember—at least not since my Army days. However, that doesn't mean a whole heckuvalot."

Matt frowned.

"Or two, he could have offed himself after Nadine left. It's only common sense. If Nadine talked, his jig was up. Hence his desperation to get her back."

Ralph glanced Matt's way. "Go over it again. Tell me everything Aunt Allie told you."

Matt slung one foot over his knee and hooked an elbow around the open window frame. "Okay, so, whenever Horace cashed a check, and who knows where he got those, he'd drop off the half-starved Althea and baby Nadine in Carrabelle at her mother Allie's. And how long does it take to cash a check, ten minutes? They were short little visits."

Ralph slowed the truck to plow through a wide puddle from yesterday's rain. "Sounds just like the old scumbag." Ralph held back the crude word he was thinking.

"And Allie never knew when Horace would show up—but it was always at a time when Daddy Bentley was at work. And Horace, who always carried a rifle, never uttered a word to Allie. His only communication was with Althea in the form of curt hand signals. Very controlling, according to Aunt Allie."

"Pathetic," Ralph said.

"Allie would race around to feed the girls, with Althea, poor hungry thing, glancing over her shoulder the whole time, too frightened to speak but a few words. She and her child spent most of their visits eating. During one of these events, Althea slipped a handwritten note to her mama apologizing for being a rebellious teen and running away with Horace. He wasn't the fine man she thought he was."

"Dang pitiful."

"Horace must have found out about it. By the time Allie's husband saw it, noticed the mention of Marianna, and organized a posse, Horace and the family were long gone without a trace."

Ralph shook his head.

"The search party went door to door—Marianna's such a small town—and asked questions. No one they questioned recognized the name of Horace Smith. But they did say a man of his description was once fired from the boy's school there. A mean old guy who'd worked there for a long time."

Ralph lifted his foot off the gas. Ah, this was a new detail. He turned to Matt. "Are you kidding? Allie said that?"

Matt nodded.

"Well I'll be a monkey's uncle. You're sure he worked at a boy's school?"

"That's what she said."

Ralph gripped the wheel and gazed into the distance. "Yep. It's all adding up now. It's all adding up."

"Right about here," Ralph said, studying the landscape to his left. He slowed, easing the tires along the route and keeping the motor quiet. He pointed as they passed a grandaddy cypress, "Check that out. Here's where we turn off." Ralph left the path and plowed through the tall grass and between medium-sized bushes. He slowed near a stand of young cypress trees and nudged his front grill up against them, his headlights buried against their feathery green foliage. "Don't want the sun's glare to help him spot us if he's out there," he whispered.

Above the canopy, though, ominous clouds eclipsed the sun, and a low wind rustled the treetops.

"Dang if these storms aren't comin' earlier and earlier," he said.

Just in front of them, below their special parking spot, a grassy bank sloped sharply down to a tributary of clear shallow water. According to Nadine, if Ralph remembered things right, the water was shallow and wide enough for a Jeep or truck to navigate from here to the camp. But today wasn't the day. They'd walk in with extreme caution.

He put his finger against his lips to silence Matt and eased his door open. "Don't let it slam," he whispered. "Weapon," he said, pointing under the seat. "And boots in the back."

This morning with Zeke's permission, Ralph had borrowed two pairs of white fisherman's boots off Zeke's boat. They would allow the men to walk upstream toward the headspring. And there, based on certain rock formations they'd verify pretty quick whether this was the right spot or not.

It seemed to be.

Matt buckled on his leather holster and reached into the back of the truck for the boots. "My aim's fairly good, Ralph, but that's only on the practice range. Nothing like this." In this situation he was more than happy to follow the leader.

"You'll be fine. Just protect yourself and keep from gettin' shot by the crazy man."

At the base of the riverbank, Ralph eased into the water, the metal detector tucked up under his arm like a rifle. He caught Matt's eye and touched a finger to his lips. "No noise," he mouthed and then pointed at his feet and leveled his hand. Nothing.

Matt gave him a thumbs-up and stepped behind him into the stream.

As slow as snails, they pushed through the shin-deep water. Any deeper and the water could overflow their boots.

After half a mile of shoving through the water, Matt's thighs began to ache. But Ralph, a man on a mission with a tough military physique, didn't seem bothered. Coral should be proud of her dad. So Matt ignored his legs and concentrated on the tunnel of vegetation, buzzing wildlife, and submerged vines drifting in the chilly current. He could have been a soldier in the Vietnam War.

A jay squawked along the right bank and flew across the water above Ralph's head. Matt wondered about Ralph's comment just now about things adding up and what Ralph knew that he didn't.

He pushed on.

"We could drive this creek," Ralph said. "But once the water narrows, it deepens, and you can't drive any farther. At that point, we search for a cutover on the opposite bank. That's where Horace drove his old Army surplus Jeep out of the water."

Matt imagined the Jeep as he focused his eyes along the bank. He used to consider those old green Army Jeeps pretty cool. Not anymore. Not if Horace had one.

But when his gaze returned to Ralph, Matt's blood ran cold.

Ralph stood frozen in mid-step. His eyes searched the left bank while his hand reached smoothly toward his holster. He slid out the gun and cocked it.

A jay called out. But Ralph didn't flinch.

He raised his barrel toward the greenery.

Matt followed suit, drawing his pistol and cocking it.

The leaves stirred and then parted.

20

Sol woke up in a tight knot with sun shining over him. His muscles were stiff and sore. At least he was warm now. He couldn't remember when the sun had felt so good. By the looks of things it had to be late morning. His limbs ached as he crawled to his hands and knees and tried to stand. But a fresh wave of vertigo hit and sent the woods into a spin. He retched, not knowing which end was up, but nothing came out. Eventually, the dizzy spell faded, and still nauseated, he stood and grabbed hold of the large tree. This was no way to start the day.

It was time to find his way out and get back to the road. At least out on the road, he could hitchhike.

Ralph held the gun steady as a doe's head, and then her neck, appeared through the foliage of the creek bank. He lowered his gun. She spotted the men and startled but held her ground. Apparently unafraid, her ears flicked, and she took a small step forward into the mud and then the water. Only then did her fawn appear beside her. They dipped their shiny black noses into the stream's surface and drank, sending tiny ripples radiating their way.

Ralph let out a breath and turned back to his buddy. He shook his head as he reholstered his weapon.

Old Horace might not be so easy.

Matt watched as Ralph took one step too many and sank to his knees in water. Ralph, half-turned in Matt's direction, stood there

78

shaking his head while water bubbled noisily around his legs as it filled his boots.

And here they were trying to be quiet.

Meanwhile, the deer had bolted and disappeared.

Under other circumstances, Matt would have laughed and Ralph would have roared. But they held back, saving it for later.

They'd arrived at the spring, a deeper, narrower place. The old geezer's turn-off had to be here. Nadine must have done a pretty good job of giving directions, and Ralph did well remembering it all these years.

But, of course, he did. Ralph had twenty years of regret to replay it in his mind.

Matt continued to search the mudbank for any indication of Horace's Jeep. Just like in the jungles of Vietnam, with all this foliage, the enemy could be inches away. So could a bullet.

And then, for the second time, Ralph paused. He reached for his gun.

Matt copied as Ralph pointed his pistol to their left and edged toward the riverbank.

Stealing close to the riverbank, Ralph parted the lower leaves with his barrel. He peered left and right below the bushes, and then backed away to study the ground some more. Squatting, he lifted the lowest limbs and gave the mud another look. No passage here. Not anymore. Nothing but thicket—long since overgrown or washed away. Overhead, the sky had darkened even further.

In the meantime, without a sound, he pulled off one boot at a time and eased the water back into the creek. He motioned for Matt to trail him up the bank to the right where the undergrowth thinned, and where he stood, peering left and right through the bushes to make sure the camp was vacated. With arm motions, he indicated how they'd circle the campsite and come back around, checking everything for signs of Horace.

It took very few minutes to circle a somewhat large woodsy area and end up back at the muddy bank. "This has to be the the camp. It fits every description. And down in my bones I sense it. Let's cut across the center," he whispered, "and see what we find."

Birds flittered up in the trees as they strode a little more confidently now across the area, fairly certain nobody was there. Midway, Ralph held out his hand for Matt to stop. Up ahead was an out-of-place brushpile. He approached with careful steps, Matt behind him. Underneath the brush sat the old rusted-out Jeep. "Would you look at that," Ralph said, still speaking in low tones. He attempted to pull away a fat limb but it disintegrated in his hand. He brushed off the debris. "It's been here a while. Years, I bet. Wonder why it's covered like this."

"I guess he didn't shoot himself," Matt said. "If he was going to do that, why would he hide it?"

"So where is he?"

They circled the rotten brushpile and studied the Jeep. A thick layer of leaves filled the floorboard, and its rotten tires sank axle-deep in debris. "Maybe Horace hid it while he went somewhere. Which means he went on foot. Or by horse. But I can't imagine that. Never saw him with a horse."

They wandered over the rest of the acre and found nothing more—at least nothing that was visible. "Let's go back and take a better look at the spot where we came in, that rectangular mound down by the spring," Ralph said. "I guarantee that's the cabin."

A smaller area near the water lay surrounded by a bushy perimeter. It seemed a perfect spot for a camp. To its left sat the mound, and behind the mound rose the roots of an uprooted oak that had crashed. Its trunk now pointed toward the Jeep. Rain and weather had disintegrated its bark and washed the soil from its roots into a heap at its base.

"We can't see a thing with all this leaf litter," Matt said. "Why don't we grab a few green limbs and sweep some of it away?"

For the next twenty minutes, they made a good stab at clearing it, starting with the outer edge of the rectangular mound. Ralph regretted not throwing some tools into the truck.

So far they'd uncovered nothing at all.

The light had dimmed even more as Matt glanced up through the treetops. "Storm's just about here."

Even as he spoke, a blast of cool air whipped through the camp and rustled the lower limbs. Matt picked up his pace, but Ralph tossed away his green branch.

"Let's give this a few more minutes," Ralph said. "We ain't gonna melt. And besides, I wanna give the metal detector a little try."

"Good idea," Matt said. He'd almost forgotten about Ralph's metal detector. "Hey, man, you go ahead and try that, and I'll keep on with this. Maybe we'll both find something."

Ralph took up the detector and turned it on. He started by circling the campsite in tighter and tighter rings. "I'll work my way in," he said. "Maybe it'll squawk." He gave it a few back-and-forth swings. "So where would you hide a pot of gold, Matt?"

"I don't know," Matt said, brushing away a hefty mass of leaves. "Fork," he said, bending down to examine the cheap metal piece that now gleamed against the dirt. He tossed it into the middle of the rectangle and swept closer to the mound. "Logs." He said, "And not much left of them. It's definitely the old cabin."

"Good find, man," Ralph said, turning away from Matt and stepping around the old fallen tree. He passed by the root and *"Screeeee!"* the detector gave off a steady high-pitched tone. "Oh, man, that's the sound you wanna hear!"

Matt leaped up and raced over. "Check it out!"

They got down on their hands and knees and began digging through the sand like two dogs looking for bones.

Ralph reapplied the detector. *"Screeeee!"*

"You've got to be kidding," Matt said as Ralph heaved the gallon-sized glass jar out of the hole.

"It weighs a ton." Ralph said. He set it down to try the rusted lid. It didn't budge. "This ain't about to come off."

"We'll bust the jar, then."

"Later," Ralph said, standing. "Once we get back." He buried the jar under a pile of leaves. "I'll keep looking." Ralph snatched up the detector and continued around the camp, and except for a few more spoons and forks, he came up empty.

Back at the mound, Matt set to work again, sweeping harder than ever to get the yard bare. He'd clear the inside of the logs next. That should be interesting.

But then, raindrops began to fall, heavy and strong as a jungle monsoon. Within seconds the wind picked up and drove it like pellets against their skin. Matt dropped his branch and snatched off his shirt. He yelled over to Ralph, "You want the detector or the jar?"

Ralph handed over the detector. "Take this."

Matt, shivering now, tossed him his shirt. "Wrap it up. Gotta protect it."

Ralph tied the garment around the jar and shoved it under his arm. "If I get tired you can carry it. Our trip back ain't gonna take as long as the trip up."

Matt gave him a thumbs up, and they set off in a rapid slog down the creek.

At Tate's Hell, Matt plunged out of the creek with Ralph right behind him. They high-tailed it up the bank and made a beeline for the parked truck. The rain drove hard against the windshield as they threw in their stuff, jumped in, and slammed the doors. Matt's teeth chattered. "Think we could turn on the heater, Ralph?"

Ralph turned the key and started the engine. "Give it a minute. Take that old sweatshirt outta the back floorboard."

The jar, wrapped in Matt's wet tee shirt was now wedged between the backseat and the toolbox with the dripping metal detector across it. Crammed up under Ralph's seat was a folded gray sweatshirt. Matt yanked it out. He was more than happy to put on the raggedy thing, and thank God, it was still warm from the sunnier part of their day. "Th-thanks, Ralph," he said, sliding it on and wrapping his arms around himself.

"Ahh, gosh this feels good." Then he glanced over at Ralph in his own dripping shirt. "Don't you want this?"

Ralph waved him away. "I'll warm up in a minute." He reached behind the seat and pulled the cooler toward him. In it were sandwiches and bottles of water. He tossed one of each to Matt. "This'll help."

The items were chilled, but Matt took them. He opened the sandwich, a good looking fish sandwich created down at the restaurant, probably this morning. "Looks good, Ralph. Thank you."

"Made those before it got busy this morning. Glad I went ahead and stuck the cooler in the truck, or we might have forgotten it."

They laughed at the truth of the statement and then ate in silence for a few minutes as the rain drummed and the truck warmed up. It didn't take long for the cab's windows to get steamy and for Ralph to crack a window.

"Ralph, I'm curious about that blue-haired girl down at the restaurant—I'm pretty sure she's the one I saw last night over at Millie's Cabin Three."

Ralph made a sour face and took another bite, speaking around it as he chewed. "That, my friend, is Delia. A big mistake."

Matt frowned, waiting for more.

"I told Millie," Ralph said, and swallowed, chasing it with water. "I told Millie I'd hire the first waitress that came along. And lo and behold, what shows up at my door? This blue-haired thing that flirts with every Joe and Harry that comes in. Even Jack and Larry, Matt. Even Jack and Larry."

"That's bad, man. You've gotta do something about her."

"Tell me about it." Ralph took another bite. "And Millie's none too pleased. But I'm workin' on it. I am."

Matt had another question. "On a different subject, what you said a while ago about things falling into place—what did you mean by that?"

Ralph nodded, chewing. "Yeah. That boys' school…" His expression took on a faraway look as the rain eased up. "Well…" Ralph popped the rest of his sandwich in his mouth and wiped off the inside of the windows with the side of his arm. He situated himself behind the wheel and put the vehicle in reverse.

Only when they'd surged through the standing water and reached the ruts did Ralph speak again. "There were reports a while back— the old place—the boys' school—is shut down now. It was up in the panhandle—Dozier, or something like that, a reform school— where they were finding bodies. Buried bodies. Fifty or so kids. Maybe even more."

"So you think maybe Horace…"

"That ain't his name, I'm sure."

"So you think maybe he was on the run."

Ralph pointed backward with his thumb. "Any better place than that back there to hide out in? But I wouldn't let on to Coral or her grandma."

Matt shook his head. "Absolutely not."

21

Sol rubbed the sweat off his sunburned face. After what felt like hours of weaving through the maze of palmettos and underbrush with no idea which way the highway or civilization was, his head throbbed and his stomach growled. All through the day he'd yelled out, "Help!" But pain shot through his head, and the sound of his voice bounced like a mere child's around the woods.

And now his arms hung limp and weary from swatting at mosquitoes along his tormented legs and arms, and scratching bites up under his shirt. He was ready to drop. But he didn't dare.

He trudged on, aiming for a particular dead tree up ahead. A hopeful place to drop and rest. The one last night had worked out well. But these dead snags all looked identical, and he hoped he hadn't gone in circles only to end up at the same one.

It wasn't. The clearing around it, smaller than the previous one, was surrounded by bushes—bushes loaded down with tiny blueberries. "Oh, man." He reached for a berry, gave it taste and then paused. He looked up into the sky. "I guess, God, I better thank You. Thank You for this food!"

He stood there eating until he could stand no more. Then he sat down in the shade and continued his feast wondering if his lips were stained blue. He looked up in the sky. "Not that I'm ungrateful. But I hope I don't have any ill effects from all this."

Eventually, Sol took off his shirt, filled it the best he could with the bounty, and then tied it up for later. Curling up on the grass beneath the tree, he indulged in a short nap. The mosquitoes didn't seem to be as bad right here. He woke to find his energy renewed. So he stood. No need to waste the daylight. He hung the bag over his shoulder and with some regret gave up his bounteous spot—in search of water.

Along the way, he stopped to look back up into heaven. "God, I guess I ought to ask for Your help. I don't know how to get out of this place. So, would You help me? And I'm sorry. I'm sorry for my whole rotten life. I really am."

When twilight fell, Sol found himself still lost. He debated whether to empty his stash of berries onto some leaves and put his shirt back on for protection against the mosquitoes, or to go ahead and eat the fruit all at once. He thought of the problems that came with eating too much fruit. But so far he'd had no physical reaction to it. So he chose to go ahead and eat.

He settled at the base of another dead tree—probably killed by lightning—and reasoned that lightning wasn't supposed to strike the same place twice. After all, last night had worked out just fine. So Sol untied the knot in his shirt full of berries and hunkered down against the tree with it laid across his lap and the berries exposed. He looked forward to finishing them off so he could wear his shirt again.

He imagined his friend Term there with him and how he'd certainly share the berries with him. Maybe Term would know how to build a fire, and they could sit around it and talk about old times. Sol laughed out loud. Old times were mere days ago. And then he thought about his mom and the way she used to tell him God was always near. "I know You can hear me, God. And I wish I did have someone to talk to," he said. "I'd sure enjoy some company."

Sol took a pinch of berries and began to nibble them one by one while at the same time imaging God next to him. He wondered if the feeling he sensed was actually God with him. He closed his eyes to enjoy it.

Sniff. Sniff.

Sol's eyes flew open, and he turned toward the sound.

His jaw dropped. There stood three, four, no five deer with pointy hooves and big brown eyes watching him. And these were big deer.

Sol didn't know what to do. Deer didn't bite, he was sure of it. But they could step on a person with those sharp little feet. He probably didn't need to worry, though, since he'd never heard of deer stepping on people.

He tossed a blueberry at the tallest one. "Here, wanna berry?"

The whole group jumped back a step but didn't leave. They leaned right back in. He held another berry in his hand. "Wanna berry? I was just thinking of Term and how I'd share these with him. So how about you? You want one?"

Sol held his breath. The bravest deer stepped forward and carefully nibbled the berry.

"I-I-I've heard deer are curious," he said. "Come on in, everybody, and sit down. I've got more berries."

The deer remained standing as he continued feeding them. Eventually, the berries ran out. "That's all. I'm sorry," he said and opened his hands to show them. They nuzzled his empty fingers. Like big dogs, they stepped even closer and sniffed his bandage, his shirt, and his body.

And then one by one, with their white tails flicking and ears twitching, the deer lay down around him.

All Sol could do was cover up with his shirt in his arms and snuggle down among them, absorbing their warmth.

"This is so amazing, God," he whispered. "Thank You. And please don't think I'm not grateful. I am. But I still want You to get me out of here."

22

Matt called me early the day Dad was set to take me to Tate's Hell. He wanted to take an early morning walk along the beach with me before he got started for the day on Millie's log. Zeke's boat wasn't going out, so Matt planned to make good use of his time.

"I think you're enjoying that work," I teased as we held hands and strolled barefoot down the sand. We'd left our shoes up by the ramp.

He laughed as he bent to pick up a shell and toss it far out into the water. "It's not bad, really."

"In that case, I won't feel guilty running off to Tate's Hell with Dad and Jessica."

We stopped at our favorite beach turn-around point, a pile of driftwood. Matt wanted pictures and had me sit on the largest piece while he took a few selfies of us together. Then he stepped back to take several of me alone.

Before I stood, he leaned in and looked me in the eye. "I can't bear spending the day without you, Coral." He kissed me as he reached for my hand. "But now, with these pics, I can have you with me all day."

"Aww, that's so sweet. I'll miss you, too," I said as we turned and headed back with the sun in our faces. I'd never been so blessed.

Within minutes, we had our shoes on again and were headed back to town along the side of the road. We passed The Captain's Table parking lot, already filled with cars, and I wondered if Millie would be getting some extra waitress help anytime soon. She'd often complained about working too hard.

We stopped at the crest of the bridge, another of our favorite spots, and watched the morning activities of Carrabelle's fishermen and dock workers nearby. "I love this place," I said.

He squeezed my hand, and we tore ourselves away from the scene. At the other end of the bridge, we crossed the highway and aimed for Grandma Allie's where Dad would soon be picking up Jessica and me.

But as we passed Millie's, out wandered a girl with a turquoise wig from the other side of the cabins. She paused near an old black vehicle parked along the sidewalk to the left of Millie's cabin.

As we passed, she opened the car door and then turned to stare at Matt. "Mm, mm, mm," she said, eyeing Matt as if he were a dessert. "There you are again, you big handsome hunk." She winked across her shoulder at him and climbed in. "See you later, honey."

Matt's jaw muscles tensed, and neither one of us said anything until we reached the front of the store.

"Who was that?" I finally said.

Matt blew out a breath and shook his head as if there were no words. He didn't seem too pleased about her.

"You don't want to know."

"She's actually living over there?" I asked.

His face told me all I needed to know.

I couldn't believe Millie would rent to her.

As soon as Matt left me at the store, Dad arrived and Jessica and I climbed into his truck. The trip to see my mom's old place, the place she lived until she was fourteen, kept me from stewing long about that awful girl with the turquoise-blue hair. I shoved it onto the shelf in the back of my mind as I clung to the seat and passenger window to keep from getting tossed around.

Dad, Jessica, and I all sat in the front seat as he navigated the soggy route through Tate's Hell. Dad had taken the time to come up here yesterday and scope the place out. He *didn't want any surprises,* he said.

The truck's giant tires flew along the ruts and sprayed mud from yesterday's storm over the bushes.

Jessica and I traded looks.

I learned one new thing about Dad and his driving today. Nothing slowed his aggressive pace.

"Good thing we came today, ladies," Dad said. "Another day of rain and these puddles would be even deeper."

I'd begged and begged him to take me out to the old place, and last night on the phone, he'd finally agreed. "All right, then. When do you want to go?"

"The first chance we can," I said. "How about in the morning?"

He laughed and crossed his arms. "You don't quit, do you? You're just like your mother."

I'd never thought about it. I guess Mama *was* persistent. She had a lot of things to overcome in her short life. She had her chance to quit on me before I was born, and she didn't.

"Matt coming along?" he wanted to know.

"He would, but he's already given his word to help Millie with that downed tree."

So I'd called Jessica while she was at work and invited her.

"Please come with us," I told her, not wanting to be alone. Of course, there was Dad, but that wasn't the same as a buddy.

Jessica and I, like sisters these days, shared everything, our histories included.

"Are you kidding?" Jessica said. "I wouldn't miss that." And she rearranged her nursing schedule to make it happen.

And now, with every bump, I was reminded of how glad I was to have her along. Real glad. We'd have a lot to talk about later.

"I'm still not crazy about the idea," Dad said. "It's not a good place."

On the way, I noticed Jessica seemed a bit subdued. Dad's hesitancy was rubbing off on her, or like me, she was probably a little nervous about what we'd find.

Dad plunged through an extra deep puddle, and we shrieked as it bounced us off the seat.

"Sorry, girls," Ralph said. "Didn't mean to hit that."

I faked a moan. "I think I'm going to need a chiropractor."

Dad and Jessica laughed.

Along the way we passed many flooded areas where sunlight sparkled off the water between spiky grasses and little yellow wildflowers. Each little meadow, surrounded by tall pines or dense palm thickets seemed like a scene from a picture book. But to our left, loomed a dark and ugly sky, like it had for the last several days.

"Ya'll just hang on," Dad said as he dodged another hole and jostled us again.

I knew little about my family, but what I did know was that my grandfather, Horace Smith, was a violent man who mistreated my mother as a child and probably murdered my grandmother, his wife.

That's all Dad would tell me about him.

"Can't you give me more?" I had asked.

"I wish I could," he answered, "but that's about it."

It wasn't clear whether that's all he knew or if he was holding back for other reasons. The little bit I'd pieced together made me squirm, and this place we were headed to was the story's epicenter.

"Down at the camp—and I don't believe anyone would call it a home," he said, "is where Horace killed Nadine's mama. Supposedly. Nadine didn't witness it. And there never was a body. So we can't be a hundred percent sure. But Nadine swore she just knew what had happened when her mama never came back."

"And a long time ago Grandma Allie dreamed he killed her," I said.

"Yeah, she told me that too. But Nadine was a young child," Dad said, "and you know how children are. She could have been confused, or her mama could have died in childbirth, a sickness, or even a snakebite without her dad explaining it to her. After all, the camp was way out in the middle of the swamp with no access to doctors. How would a child know for sure?"

I thought about what he said, but I knew a twelve-year-old isn't a baby. I think my dad was just trying to make me feel better.

"Don't be disappointed if there's not much to see at the campsite, ladies."

Dad slowed near a cluster of seven sabal palms that stood together, their tops leaning away from each other like a little family playing ring-around-the-rosy. He pointed it out. "First marker."

We continued along the state park's roads. "You know how landscapes can change," he said. "But the few markers your mama told me about are still in place." He lifted his foot off the gas and pointed to the odometer. "We go by distance now. Tate's Hell has only been a state park for around thirty years," Dad said. "But it's common knowledge they still have trouble with squatters today, just like back in the day when your mama's family was there. I guess that's why the camp is so well hidden."

I couldn't imagine the camp, but I could picture my grandfather going house to house with a rifle and threatening anyone and everyone to hand over his daughter. I envisioned him growing angrier and angrier when they said nothing—because nobody knew a thing about it. Not even my dad's father.

But Ralph, my nineteen-year-old father knew.

Because he was hiding her on the third floor above his dad's restaurant.

Protective custody, I guess, and that made him a hero. I was proud of him.

I peeked around Jessia at his big strong arms. He kept in shape, like a soldier. But at the same time, he was soft-hearted, kind to cats and people. And a hero of course. So far, that's about all I knew about him, and I liked it all.

He pointed to the left where a white heron lifted into the air. Its sunlit wings blazed like white neon against a hard gray sky. So lovely.

I heaved a long sigh that had nothing to do with the bird.

Jessica gave me a reassuring look.

Despite my earlier excitement, as we drove deeper into the woods, my nerves began to jangle. Jessica must have sensed it. She patted my hand.

After a while, our truck forked left along ruts that led through a swampy bog. "There'll be a crossing back here," Dad said.

I wrapped my arms around myself and squeezed away the shivers as the truck's front end battled its way through tall weeds and water.

He slowed to a crawl and twisted left to lean out the window. "See that back there? That stand of cypress trees. Take note of that one, the grandaddy. Boy, look at that thing. Another marker. Once you see that, the camp's not far. We'll enter the water just past that thicket." He pressed on the gas again. Jessica and I gripped the dash as the tires descended the steep bank and leveled out in a wide but shallow creek. He kept on driving.

Near what he said was a spring, we rolled up another bank into a clearing and stopped.

Dad turned off the engine. It cooled down with clicks and tics, and for several seconds nobody spoke.

I closed my eyes and listened to the things my mother would have listened to—the twitter and squawk of birds high in the canopy and the overwhelming racket of cicadas all around us.

My dad cracked open his door, and I opened my eyes.

He pointed out the low rotting remains of a campsite in the middle of the clearing. "There it is," he said.

The place where my mother and her mother were held captive.

Where one died and the other one escaped.

In this dense forest of Tate's Hell only the barest flecks of light penetrated the gloom. I hoped it wasn't this overgrown when Mama was here. I stepped to the damp earth beside the truck and gazed around at Mama's childhood camp. "My poor mother," I whispered as Jessica climbed out behind me.

"You okay, Coral?" Dad asked from his side as he pocketed his keys. I nodded, swallowed, and rubbed a chill off my arms despite summer temperatures. This place wasn't one I'd want to be in alone.

Jessica, wordless, stood at my elbow. She turned in a full circle, her gaze on the area around us.

"What's your impression?" I whispered. "Your true honest opinion."

She gave a nervous laugh and peered back at the dangling vines through which the truck had just blasted out of the creek. Water still dripped from the vines and the vehicle's chassis. "You mean other than a dead tree, a bunch of overgrowth, and that pile of stuff?"

Nothing like avoiding my question. I knew that if I sensed its creepiness, Jessica did too, but she probably wouldn't admit it right now.

She might later, though, when just the two of us could talk about it.

"Wanna take pictures?" she asked.

I frowned and shook my head. One good look was memory enough.

We girls traversed the small clearing to the remains of the old cabin with my dad following behind. "How'd you find this camp, Dad, after all that time?"

He shrugged.

The cabin's ruins consisted of a rotten rectangle of collapsed material no more than two feet high. It seemed no more than a pile of moldy leaves and sticks—a big compost pile. And the whole place smelled of decay.

Dad kept to himself and allowed Jessica and me our space, but he did offer one thing. "These walls had to be palm logs," he said, addressing its four-sided border. "Under the right conditions, especially wet ones, they're quick to disintegrate."

For a few minutes, we contemplated and discussed what the site might have looked like back then and how the family could have possibly survived. Under all this shade, it didn't seem as if it could grow much food. But then, landscapes do change. The trees could have been cleared back then.

A cool breeze rustled the lower limbs of the thick foliage. The shade deepened even more.

Dad peered up through the canopy. "Not to rush you, ladies, but the sun's gone. I'll be down at the stream a minute while you finish up your lookin' around." He strolled down the sloped bank.

There wasn't much left to examine but the back side of the debris pile. "We should at least walk around it," I said.

"I'm glad you found your dad," Jessica said as he stepped out of earshot. We skirted the mound, and she gazed back to where he'd disappeared behind the truck. "It drives me nuts to not know who my own father is."

Lately, the topic of Jessica's unknown heritage had come up, and we'd both prayed for God to give her some insight.

"Yeah. But anything's possible," I told her. "You know how things can change overnight."

"I know," she sighed. "You sound just like your Grandma Rosella."

I chuckled. "Be patient and give God time to work it out. You know He's listening. But you can't tell what He's doing behind the scenes. And just maybe…"

I raised my hand and dropped it again. But I didn't tell her what I was thinking—that sometimes God says no. And it's for our own good.

I, for one, wished I didn't even know about my grandfather. "Jessica, I really hate knowing I'm the grandchild of a murderer. I wish Horace was a good ol' grandpa, a storybook character. One I could be proud of. Some things I didn't need to know."

My chest knotted as I stared around the moldy space with its cloying overgrowth. The truth of this camp and my evil grandfather weighed heavy on me, like a lead blanket. If only I could shuck it off.

Enough of this talk. I wanted to steer the conversation to something good. For both our sakes. I pointed out the perimeters of the old cabin and blurted, "I bet there's a dish or something under that pile that belonged to Mama or her mama." But as soon as the words left my mouth, I knew better.

She perked up. "Your dad might have a shovel in the truck."

"No. No. No. Forget it. Really, with my family's violent history, an object from here would just creep me out."

But she wasn't done talking about her father. "Maybe I should just keep pestering my mother about it."

So much for changing topics.

"You know," she kept on, "if I ask her again and again, like every single day, she might give in."

"She has her reasons," I said, "but that's up to you. I wouldn't. What about DNA testing?"

She shrugged. "I don't know."

Fat pellets of rain began to hit the vegetation, and I turned away and motioned her forward. "C'mon, kiddo. Enough of this place. Let's go."

Boom!

I jumped. Thunder rattled the woods, and a frantic wind whipped the branches. "It's coming," I yelled.

I turned, expecting to see Jessica right behind me, but she was still glued to the spot I'd just left.

"Hold on," she said, parting the bushes, her eyes focused on the ground.

The wind slackened for a moment as Dad jogged up from the creek below. "Hey! Let's get outta these trees," he hollered.

I whirled around to my friend.

"Jessica! Come on."

Jessica held up a finger, and I rushed back to see what she'd found. Back at the truck, Dad climbed in and started the engine.

"Hey, just a sec," she said, pointing under the foliage. "When the wind whipped up, I spotted something down there." She dropped to her knees and ducked under the leaves. "I thought it was a bowl, or—shoot, where's a light when you need it?"

The passage between the ruins and the foliage was narrow, and her body blocked the view. I couldn't see a thing.

"There it is." She broke off a twig and set to work digging. Her voice was muffled under the branches. "Stems everywhere, but I'm getting it. Are you sure you don't want a souvenir, Coral?"

"Let me..." I tried to step around her to see.

But she blocked me with her hand. "Wait. Nope. Juuust a ..."

Then she scrambled back out like she'd seen a snake and stumbled to her feet. I stepped back to keep from getting knocked over. Breathless, she brushed off her hands and turned me toward the truck. "Nevermind," she said, and nudged me forward. "It's ugly and broken and you couldn't fix it. And like you said, it would give you the creeps."

The gust of wind whipped my hair in front of my face. The pelting in the bushes intensified. Drops of rain hit our heads. In mere seconds it would let loose and pour.

Boom!

"Run!" I yelled and raced for the truck.

Back at the vehicle I flung open the door and let Jessica climb in first.

Dad was first to speak. "What was all that?" he asked.

"Oh, Jessica found..."

But my friend surprised me. "Don't go yet," she said. "Can you go take a look at something—with your flashlight?"

"You said it was broken," I reminded her. "Let's not worry about it."

She ignored me. "Just in case Coral wants it. I couldn't see very well with all these dark clouds."

Dad glanced through the windshield at the weather. Then back at Jessica.

She hadn't taken her eyes off him. "Please?"

Resolute, he grabbed his phone, opened the door, and stepped out.

"You'll get wet, Dad," I insisted. "Just let it go."

Rain spattered the windshield as he eased the door shut and crossed the bare ground to the back of the ruins where we'd just been. He pointed to the spot and turned back to Jessica for confirmation. She nodded and perched on the edge of her seat as Dad ducked down in the same place she'd been.

When he came up again, he pocketed his phone and stared down at the bushes. Then he brushed off his hands and returned to the truck.

As he passed by the front of the truck with a blank expression, he traded a look with Jessica.

He swung open the door and stepped up, putting the truck in reverse, and making a three-point turn. Before he struck out through the water, he heaved a sigh and then turned my way, but not before catching Jessica's eye again.

"Good catch, Jessica," he said. And then he addressed me. "Coral, I'm sorry, honey, the dish is no good. And Jessica was right. It's too broken to fix."

From the looks on their faces, he and Jess felt bad for my lost opportunity.

"Really, I'm fine," I said. "I didn't need a memento. It would only remind me of Horace and his violence. Especially a broken one."

They studied my face.

I shrugged. "But thank you for checking on it."

The rain poured, and aside from the slapping wipers, the wash of water beneath the Chevy as it rolled back up the stream, and the pelting against the metal roof, our ride back to town remained fairly quiet.

And all the while, I wondered why Dad and Jessica felt so bad about some broken dish.

23

Ralph drove pell-mell back to town from Tate's Hell. The rain had slowed to mere sprinkles, and as he dropped off the girls at Aunt Allie's and swung around behind the restaurant, all he could think about was calling Matt to tell him what they had found at the campsite.

The sun burst through the clouds as he shifted the truck into park and whipped out his cell phone. He hadn't even turned off the engine.

But static crackled in his ears. Matt picked up, though, so Ralph gave it a shot. "Hey, bud," he said, "got a second?"

The only garbled words that made it through the static were *cutting limbs* and *broken chainsaw.*

Broken tools—of course. Ralph had recognized how handy Matt was and had dug them out for the log work. But they were old and worn. Together they could have made short work of the tree. But not if the tools weren't working. Ralph was to be blamed for not going down there and helping the kid.

He shook his head at the crackling phone. Dang lousy time for the cell towers to mess up. He gave it another try. "Can you hear me?"

He glanced at his watch. Barely eleven.

Nevertheless, he continued. "Millie's coming up to the restaurant in a minute. Seeing how it's midweek, she and Larry and Jack can handle things without me this afternoon. Can you be ready in ten minutes?"

Once again, the response was gnarled.

So Ralph raised his voice. "I'll be there in ten minutes."

"What?"

"Put. Up. Your. Tools," Ralph yelled. "You're going up to Tallahassee with me. We'll get lunch on the way."

It was late morning when Dad dropped Jessica and me back at the front of Grandma Allie's store. The rain had fizzled out. The grandmas were busy shelling peas around the now-cold Franklin stove, so we said hello and slipped on past them to change clothes and have an early bite of lunch before Jessica went to work.

I fixed an extra sandwich and a peach for Matt.

All I wanted was to unburden myself to him about the horrible place we'd just visited and the way it made me feel and the evil I sensed. However, knowing how busy he was, I decided to settle for a brief text for now.

But my phone was nowhere to be found. "Jessica, have you seen my phone?"

We retraced our steps but came up empty. "I'll dial you," she said.

But silence.

"You had it back in the truck."

"And I never took it out. Guess I'll get it later."

The feelings I wanted to express should be done face to face anyway—with hugs. I needed some.

More than anything I needed Matt's hugs.

Matt clicked off the phone with Ralph. With his back to the log, he lifted the bottom of his tee-shirt to wipe another round of sweat and sawdust off his face. Between the dull chainsaw chain and tough wood of Millie's oak, he'd made very little progress this morning. Then just before Ralph called, the chain broke.

He pulled the tee-shirt over his head and balled it up to wipe the sweat off his torso. Then he turned around to gather up the tools and nearly jumped out of his skin.

There on the log sat Delia with her hands on her knees posed like Betty Boop in the shortest of all shorts.

He froze, speechless.

"Ooh, la la!" she cooed, looking him up and down. Spread out on the log was a red and white tablecloth with two drinks and twin subs. For who?

Matt gritted his teeth. His nose flared. "What's this?" he said.

"Mmm, mmm, mmm!" she said, her eyes trained on him.

He flapped open the wadded shirt, yanked it back over his head, and then made an effort to modulate his voice and gather his thoughts. He extended a hand toward the food. "I'm sorry, miss. I can't be having a picnic out here with you."

Undeterred, she kept her smile and batted her eyes. "I thought maybe we'd enjoy a little lunch and spend some time together."

This girl was from some other world.

"Maybe you misunderstand. I've got a girlfriend. And I can't be out here with you. At all."

She dipped her head and looked up with a grin. "Maybe you should rethink that little relationship."

He stood there with his arms crossed, not knowing what else to say that would get through to the girl. "I'm sure there are lots of other guys in town to choose from. And you won't have any trouble striking up a friendship—just not with me—and not in this way."

She sat there swinging her foot, seemingly unfazed.

He uncrossed his arms. "Listen, not to be rude, but I've gotta go." He turned, stepped toward his cabin, and ascended the steps with a sigh. Once he closed the door behind him, he leaned his back against its wooden panels. What was this girl thinking?

He only had ten minutes to get cleaned up. He glanced at his phone. Nope. Make that eight. His hands trembled as he sent Coral a brief text before his shower.

`Lunch with Ralph. Going to Tallahassee.`

Keys in hand, Millie opened the door of her cabin. And there she stopped, eyes wide, as Delia arranged a red checkered tablecloth over the log. *What in the world?*

Matt, talking on his phone with his back to Delia, seemed oblivious to her presence.

Delia, meanwhile, swayed to and fro laying out her Subway lunch for two on top of the cloth. Then she took a seat on the log and posed.

Millie gasped. *The little predator.* She could hardly believe her eyes.

Instead of leaving for work, Millie waited to see what Matt would do. Surely, he wouldn't fall for this tramp.

When Matt turned around and saw the girl, Millie snorted. The look on his face! Total shock. *Good boy, Matt.*

She couldn't hear a thing the girl said, but her body language said plenty. Millie grinned when Matt told her he had a girlfriend.

The girl said a few more things. Then he turned and walked away. *Good boy, Matt.*

The blue-haired girl, as dumb as a cockroach, seemed unbothered by his reaction. She remained in that provocative pose even after he left. Then she gathered her things and prissed away to her own cabin. As if nothing had happened.

The nerve! Ralph shouldn't have hired her.

Millie stepped on through the doorway and locked up.

When I rounded the corner of Bentley's Store and glimpsed the scene in front of Matt's cabin, I froze in my tracks. My heart sank to the dirt as I stood there beside the front post.

I took in the scene at the log, the tablecloth, the blue-haired girl, her posture in those shorts, and the food—for two...

...and Matt standing there talking to her.

I edged out of sight, trying to sort it out.

Shoot. I wish I had my phone.

Tears welled up in my eyes.

Everything about that girl was wrong. And he was most definitely in her sights.

Surely, Matt wasn't turning his head for—for *that.*

24

Sol woke up on the sand with the sun bearing down on his face and cramps ripping through his guts. The stink of his own gas mixed with the smell of warm earth next to his nostrils. Another pang hit, and a tear rolled across his nose. He winced and tightened into a ball.

Never, ever, had he suffered this kind of agony. He comforted himself with the thought that there could be worse things—like having a baby—or getting burned alive by natives in a jungle—and there had to be some end to this experience.

Sol clutched a sand-laden root as another blade worked its way through his intestines.

He distracted himself by thinking of the deer he saw last night and wondered if they weren't standing behind him now, watching. And then he began to wonder whether the deer had actually been a figment of his imagination, some side-effect or hallucination from his head injury. But when he opened his eyes, there lay his poor crumpled shirt, half buried among the pointy hoof prints.

Sol gasped and tightened as a new wave twisted his gut. He held his breath—and then when he could hold back no longer—a warmth drenched his rear.

Prickled in sweat, but somewhat relieved, he knew this had to be the blueberries—or the water he'd been drinking from the mudpuddles. But what choice did he have?

The attack on his innards began to let up. But the mess on his back end burned like acid. He sat up and leaned against the tree and, as if his nose hadn't already confirmed it, he checked his britches. "Gaaa!" A loud stream of cuss words echoed through the woods.

And then they faded. Sol needed help.

Well. Hadn't God helped him last night?

Sol laid his arms across his knees and opened his hands. "See this mess, God? I know you see me down here. And I don't think you're laughing. So, can I just get a drink of water and wash up? Please?"

He sat there on his bum and listened for God's voice as the wind stirred the pines. The soft sound mixed with the distant twitter and squawk of birds. Distant clouds reminded him that rain might return. But he could not hear God's answer.

"Help meeeeee!" he begged. And this time he realized the yelling didn't hurt his head. At least that was improved.

He stumbled to his feet, dislodged his shirt from the sand, and shook it out. Once he put it on, he stripped off his pants and underwear and cleaned himself with leaves as best he could. Whatever the plants were, he hoped they didn't give him a rash.

Somewhere along the path, he grew tired of the stink and found a long stick to carry his soiled clothes.

25

Ralph climbed into his truck and started the engine when a ring tone in the seat next to him sounded off. He glanced over at the pink phone.

One of the girls must have left it this morning. Better stop off at Aunt Allie's before I pick up Matt.

He climbed out of his truck and up the steps but found nobody stirring. "Anybody home?" he hollered, opening the screen door and stepping in.

"In here, Ralph," Aunt Allie called, her voice frail.

He turned left and passed through the parlor to the store to find Aunt Allie and Miss Rosella seated by the old stove shelling peas—peas he'd ordered for Aunt Allie earlier in the week, a big seller at her store. Not that she had more than a dozen customers a week. He'd like to find a way to increase her business. But that was something for another day.

"Hey, there," he said. "You ladies all right today?"

They nodded and assured him all was well.

"Truck's still runnin' out back so I can't stay. But here's one of the girls' phones if you'll pass it along. It got left behind this morning."

"Glad to," Aunt Allie said, reaching out to take it. "It's about time for lunch. Would you like to stay for a bite to eat?"

"No, no. Thank you just the same. Like I said, I left the truck runnin', and I've gotta go tend to some business."

He bid the ladies good-bye and stepped back through the building and off the back porch to discover Matt already seated in the passenger seat.

Ralph grinned and climbed in behind the wheel. "Well, look what the cat dragged in."

"Saw you drive by."

"Good timing," Ralph said.

Matt shook his head, a look of pure exasperation on his face. "I couldn't wait. Not after what just happened."

Yeah, well, wait till Matt heard what Ralph had to say.

After spotting Delia at Matt's, I didn't know what to think. I turned around and parked myself on Grandma Allie's front store steps to think it over.

A few minutes later, I leaned around the corner again, and Delia, Matt, the cloth, and the food had all disappeared. There was no way she could eat that fast.

A giant lump filled my heart.

Delia wasn't truly ugly—*except for that horrible hair and her presumptive attitude.*

She seemed just the type to hammer and hammer and hammer until she got what she wanted.

I simply could not believe her gall.

Such a devil.

And where could Matt be?

My circular thoughts fell all over themselves. I huffed out a hard sigh and stood, trying to put it out of my mind. I didn't know whether to be concerned about Matt's resolve or to just accept that Delia was being her own stupid self, and he'd ignore her.

Blue hair and all, Delia is a clown. Of course, he'd ignore her.

Shoot. After we came back from Tate's Hell, we really should have stopped by Millie's log on the way home. But with the rain and Ralph being in such a hurry and Jessica needing to get to work…

I turned and swung open the front door to the store. There sat Grandma Allie and Grandma Rosella by the stove shelling peas into baskets on their laps.

"Hey there," I said, hoping not to give away my slumpy feelings. But it didn't work.

"Sit down here, child. What's the matter?" Grandma Rosella never missed a thing about me.

What was I thinking? I should have gone around to the side door. This was going to be difficult with the two of them staring me down. No use arguing. I sat down on the old orange crate beside Grandma Rosella and leaned my elbows on my knees.

Grandma Allie pulled a basket from under her chair and threw in a handful of peas from her bushel basket. "Here, you don't have to tell us right now. But pitch in with these peas and give us a hand."

Thank goodness. I couldn't express my thoughts if I tried, at least those about Delia. I set to work shelling.

We worked in silence for a while, my thoughts about the girl so loud I could have sworn they were audible.

But I knew exactly how I felt about the old campsite. And since I didn't want to appear too brooding, I brought them up. "The campsite," I said, resting my hands on the basket, "it was awful."

Both grandmas looked my way.

"Musty, dark, and gloomy—a storm on the way. But the creepy feeling I got—went way beyond the weather."

Grandma Allie nodded. "I thought that might happen. You sorry you went?"

I gazed up at the ceiling as I turned it over in my mind. "Not really." I slid open another pod and pressed out the peas with my thumb. They rained into the basket. "That feeling, it was like a heavy sack on my back. A wet blanket, maybe. It's hard to describe. There was definitely an evil presence all around."

The grandmas traded glances.

"I'm blood related to that man, that evil, violent person. And I don't like it at all."

Grandma Rosella gave my knee a pat. "We all have garbage in our lineage. You remember what the Word says, don't you? *All have sinned and come short of the glory of God.*"

"And for the most part," Grandma Allie said, "we don't know what our ancestors were up to. We'd probably all hide our heads in shame if we did."

"I know. I'm not trying to be self-righteous."

"I know you're not," Rosella said. "But you wish you could undo it, don't you?"

I sighed and closed my eyes. "Yes."

She rested her hand on my knee and bowed her head. "Father, we pray for this child that you will cut her loose from these generational curses and evils. Set her free and give her a new beginning. Take the burden off her and give her a new life unburdened by the past. Break all the ties that bind. In Jesus' name we pray. Amen."

As I wiped the tears from my eyes, Grandma Allie followed with her own *amen*. "And we know He hears our prayer, because the Word says He came to set the captives free. And isn't that being a captive? Realizing an evil relative was in your past?"

I nodded and stood with my basket of peas. "Thank you, Grandma and Grandma. I hope you don't mind if I go and spend a little alone time."

"Not at all, "Allie said. "Hand me your basket and," she reached into her apron pocket, "I think this is yours."

"My phone! Thank you. How did you get it?"

"Ralph dropped it off."

I checked my screen as I strolled away. "Thank you."

I left the grandmas and checked my messages. Only one from Matt.

Sent around eleven, it said:

```
Lunch with Ralph. Going to Tallahassee.
```

Well, that was a relief. But then, if Delia wasn't expecting Matt, who was she waiting for?

I wondered briefly what they were up to in Tallahassee and then shrugged and plugged in the muted phone. I kicked off my shoes to take a nap.

With everything swirling around in my head, I needed to clear my thoughts.

26

Matt leaned back in the truck and crossed a foot over his knee, ready to unload his Delia-experience on Ralph. But as he opened his mouth, Ralph made a wide U-turn onto Highway 98 and spoke first.

"I apologize, Matt, but let me interrupt. What I'm about to tell you might just trump what you've got."

Matt took a deep breath and let it out. He needed to cool off anyway. "Okaaay. Everything all right?"

Ralph stepped on the gas and accelerated east, much faster than the posted forty miles per hour.

"A coupla things, Matt—and no, not exactly all right. So, listen up," he said as trees whizzed by.

Curious or not, Matt had to mention the speed limit sign. They didn't need a ticket.

Ralph let off the gas. "Sorry. Just a bit of anxiety." With hardly a pause, he dove right back into his story. "I'm not sure what to tell you first. Let's start with what we—what Jessica—found out there by the riverbank."

Matt frowned. Their own trip the day before had turned out fine, and that jar— "Was Coral okay with the place? I mean, did it upset her?"

"She wasn't elated with the setting, no." Ralph raised a thumb off the wheel and peered past it at the speedometer. Once again, he let off the accelerator. "She seems to be fine. But I don't think she realizes… Let's just say Coral thinks we found a broken bowl and left it behind. She has no idea we found a body."

Matt twisted forty-five degrees to face Ralph. "A body. You found a body?"

"A skull, at least. Whether male or female, I have no clue. We left it right where it was. But yes, there could be a body. And we have to report it. Today."

Matt blew out a breath. "Yeah, can't mess with a crime scene."

"If that's what it is. And I, for one, want to know who's dead out there. This impacts me, as well as Coral." Ralph glanced his way. "And on the way there, I have some other business to tend to."

"What about our jar?" Matt asked. "Isn't that evidence?"

Ralph gave him a look. "You know, I've given that some thought. And here's how I figure it. According to the evidence—the Jeep we found—we know it's Coral's mother's camp. And that jar's the same as her inheritance."

Matt nodded.

"Not that we have to tell anyone. And furthermore," Ralph said, "when we discovered it, we had no idea there was a skull. That came later. And after that storm—that *drencher?* No worries. Our diggings are long since washed away."

"And that skull? We can't tell Coral about it."

"I've got more," Ralph said. "But it's your turn. What happened to you just now?"

"You're right," Matt admitted, "your story does trump mine." But then he proceeded to complain about Delia and her Betty Boop antics at the log."

"What was she thinking?"

"I guess she thinks men are just a bunch of dogs," Matt said. "Cue them up, and they'll foam at the mouth. But not me. Not this man."

"Good for you," Ralph said and then changed topics. "Did I ever tell you about that barbecue place up the road here? Best one around."

"We stopping in?"

Ralph grinned. "Wouldn't pass it by."

But they didn't have time to sit down and eat. They grabbed their barbecue beef sandwiches to go. Back in the truck, Ralph located his flattened roll of paper towels behind the seat, tossed it over to Matt, and backed out of the parking lot. Half the day was gone, and besides reporting the skull, Ralph had other business at Fine China, Glitter, and Gems in Tallahassee.

"What was that other thing you mentioned?" Matt said between mouthfuls.

Ralph took a sip of sweet tea and wiped his sticky fingers on a towel. He now regretted the decision to eat as he drove.

"Well, I'm in a bit of a strain with Millie. Over that blue-haired chick. Millie is not pleased with me at all."

"Go on."

"She wants another waitress. She mentioned cutting back on Delia's hours until she's forced to quit."

"Don't look at me."

"I am looking at you, Matt. You've gotta help me."

Matt's voice rose an octave. "Are you kidding? After the stunt that girl pulled today?"

"C'mon, help me out, here, Matt."

Matt stared out the passenger window and stuffed a fry in his mouth.

Ralph could have reminded Matt his other job with Zeke was slipping away. With all this rainy weather and Zeke having to help his wife's mother up the coast with assisted living things—by the time Zeke got things squared away, his old deckhand would be back. Instead, he said, "I'm sure you could use the money."

Matt tossed him a frown. "But I'd be confined in the restaurant with that…that hussy." He shook his head. "I can't, Ralph. I just can't. Why don't you fire the girl?"

"It's not that easy. I gave my word, Matt. I promised Millie I'd hire the first person that came along. Not only that, the girl's paid her rent for the month. All because of me givin' her the job. I'm in a corner here tryin' to do right by everybody."

Matt gave him a stern look. "What? Why am I the one feeling trapped? Just cut her free."

"Whether I fire her or not, she's got that cabin for the month. Might as well get some use out of her. Can you imagine her out wanderin' the town? I'll tighten the screws. Maybe she'll up and quit. In the meantime, I need your help."

Matt shook his head and stared out the passenger window.

"Look," Ralph said, "it's just for a short time. Separate dining rooms. I'll make sure. I'm begging you. Save me from the wrath of Millie."

By the time Ralph parked his truck at the Fine China, Glitter, and Gems, he'd finally persuaded Matt to at least think about it. Matt said he'd run it by Coral and see what she thought.

"It doesn't matter that you've never waited tables before," Ralph said. "You'll catch on quick. All my customers will love you, and it'll be fun. Guaranteed you'll learn faster than Larry. And he's catching on fine."

"Hire Larry, then."

Ralph gave him the eye. "I need Larry in the kitchen." He gave Matt's shoulder a bump with his fist and opened his door.

Matt climbed out of his side of the truck.

"I knew you'd come through," Ralph told him. "You'll do great."

Glass display cases lined the perimeters of Fine China, Glitter, and Gems. Matt ambled around them and studied precious metals, diamonds, and other gems while giving Ralph plenty of space to tend to his own business.

Between the hum of the air conditioner and the hushed voices of the salesman and Ralph, he discerned very little of what was being said. Behind the glass, the irritating price tags were all flipped over to the blank side, making window shopping a futile endeavor, and Matt soon grew bored.

With Ralph taking so much time, he figured the man must be looking at engagement rings. But Ralph's negotiations were none of Matt's business, so he kept his mouth shut and took a seat on the sofa by the entrance, propping one foot across his knee.

He checked his phone. Still no response to his text to Coral. So, he tried again, this time leaving a voicemail. "You okay? I'm still in Tallahassee with Ralph. But I want to hear about your morning."

After a long wait with no answer, he leaned his head back and closed his eyes.

Before long, Ralph was jostling him. "Hey, wake up, buddy."

Matt blinked and sat up to find Ralph holding onto a pair of boxes.

He set one on the sofa and opened the lid of the other one. "Look inside here," Ralph said. "Ain't this a beaut?"

Matt peeked into the box only to find a gold-rimmed coffee cup. "A red coffee cup? That's what you came in for?" He tried to control his tone to sound more curious than shocked. But shocked he was.

"Two," Ralph said. "A matching pair." Ralph lowered his voice to a whisper. "Now let's go report that skull."

Matt didn't want to hurt Ralph's feelings, but inside, he was shaking his head. He felt sorry for Millie. Ralph seemed to be taking a mighty long time to tie the knot. From what Matt knew they'd been an item for years.

Some people.

Matt waited in the truck while Ralph checked in at the Leon County Sheriff's Department in Tallahassee. A very few minutes later he was back in the truck starting the engine.

Matt gave him a questioning look. "That was quick."

Ralph let out a breath. "Wrong jurisdiction," he said. "Gotta go down to Eastpoint."

"How far's that?"

Ralph rolled his eyes and shook his head. "Clear on the other side of Carrabelle."

An hour and a half later they pulled into the parking lot of the Franklin County Sheriff's Department and Ralph climbed out. "Might as well wait here in the truck again. Maybe we can get this thing over with."

Matt watched as Ralph entered the building.

27

For the second time that day, Matt waited in the truck at a sheriff's office as Ralph checked in to report the skull. This time it was the Franklin County Sheriff's office at Eastpoint.

After about thirty minutes, Ralph hopped back in the truck. "We're gonna wait here They'll come around from the back with the trucks," he said, as he turned on the motor and put down the windows. "They're about to follow us down there to see where the place is. I let 'em know they'd be drivin' down a stream."

"That's it?"

Ralph shrugged his shoulders. "Well, they had me describe the spot, tell why we were down there, what we did when we got there, and why we think we found a skull. Had to provide ID and sign some things, and so on. Since you weren't there when we found the skull, I didn't give 'em yours. But anyway, they got all the juicy details."

"Yeah."

"But I wasn't stupid," Ralph added.

Matt took that to mean Ralph left off details of the jar.

"Like I said, that's my daughter's inheritance."

Matt nodded again.

Two large trucks loaded up with gear soon joined Ralph, and the three vehicles set off in the direction of Carrabelle and Tate's Hell.

Matt observed as Ralph steered his truck. With two sheriff's trucks in back of him, Ralph drove in a more respectable manner with fewer risks and stuck to the speed limit.

Matt hoped Ralph's leaving out the detail of the jar wouldn't come back to bite him. But he didn't blame the man.

Meanwhile, Matt reached for his phone and texted Coral.

```
I'm still out with your dad. It might
be late when we get back. Love you,
Matt.
```

As he hit the send button it reminded him of how curt and unfriendly his and Coral's first texts were, each resenting the other for what they completely misunderstood. He'd been purposely antagonistic to her. But that was before they actually met. He chuckled. It seemed so long ago.

"What are you laughin' about?" Ralph wanted to know.

Matt smiled. "I'll tell you about it one day. And you'll enjoy the story. But not right now, not with all this going on."

He pocketed his phone returning his attention to the trip at hand. They'd reached the bank leading down to the stream.

This time, instead of hiking through the water in boots, they plunged in and drove on through.

At the campsite, the three trucks pulled up through the vines and into the narrow clearing.

The first deputy approached Ralph's door as he climbed out. "Would you walk us around the perimeter of the area you explored, sir?"

Matt accompanied Ralph and the deputy as two more followed behind marking off the area with their roll of yellow tape. To Matt it felt surreal to be in the middle of an actual investigation.

When the opportunity arose and Ralph pointed out the supposed skull to the officer, Matt leaned over and caught his first glimpse of what appeared to be the back side of it. To Matt there was no mistaking it.

The deputies scarcely commented but marked the spot with a little wire flag, as well as the Jeep over in the trees, and the rotted cabin.

Ralph stood beside the one deputy and placed the fingertips of both hands together. "So I understand you can find and identify DNA in old bones?"

"If it's the right bone and not too old," the deputy replied.

"We have a particular interest in knowing if the bones were my daughter's grandmother or grandfather," Ralph said. "Could we get some feedback?"

"If we can find a viable sample, sir, we can give you feedback, especially since your daughter's a potential relative. And then we'll need DNA from your daughter."

Matt frowned over at Ralph. They'd have to find a way to do that without letting her know about the investigation. First things first, though. The deputies had to find a valid sample here before that was needed.

"About how long will the investigation take?" Matt asked.

The deputy shook his head. "I'm not going to pretend. It takes a while. You wouldn't want to hold your breath."

"Like a month?"

The deputy chuckled. "Maybe even a year."

"Oh, man," Ralph said. "I had no idea." He turned to Matt. "We don't even need to bring this up with anybody. It's so much of a wait. What do you say we just inform them after the fact?"

"It could be less, though," the deputy said. "You never know. But when the investigation's complete, we can definitely inform you if it's a relative."

Matt took a deep breath. The time involved surprised him, too. He glanced at Ralph and wondered if they were done.

Ralph had nothing more to offer the deputies. "Like I said, the rain chased us away," Ralph said, "so we weren't here very long."

They all shook hands, and Ralph and Matt prepared to leave.

"Any chance," Matt asked, "that we could come watch you dig?"

"From a distance," a female deputy replied. "As long as you stand outside the second perimeter."

"Second perimeter?" Matt wanted to know.

"It's not up yet, but it will be, since it's public land. But the work's fairly tedious, and I doubt you'll see much."

Ralph tipped his chin in the direction of the deputies who'd strung up the yellow tape. They'd started unpacking a truck and now appeared to be setting up camp. "So, what's up with the camping equipment?"

The female deputy smiled. "From here on out we'll be keeping someone on site."

"You start tonight?"

"We start first thing in the morning."

Matt followed Ralph as they bid the crew good-bye and left the site. He sure wouldn't want to be the person spending the night out here.

It was still daylight when Matt and Ralph returned from Tate's Hell, so Matt stopped by Aunt Allie's.

"Afternoon, Matt," she said, swinging open the back porch screen door and welcoming him in. "Have a chair. Rosella's taking a nap right now. And so is that sweet girl of yours. Where in the world have you been all day?"

Matt pulled out a seat and sat at the table. "Here there and yonder, you know. Ralph had some personal business up in Tallahassee and asked me to go."

"I won't pry then," she said. "You doin' all right? Would you like some pie?"

Matt welcomed the pie and her lack of prying. But he stuck to his and Ralph's plan and kept mum regarding the investigation.

Aunt Allie served him a blueberry version of poor man's pie and offered him seconds when he polished off the first.

"That's mighty nice of you," he told Aunt Allie, "but thank you anyway. Since Coral's asleep, Ralph and I could use this time to work on Millie's log. When Coral wakes up, would you mind letting her know I'll come back later?"

She took his dish and fork. "Of course. You run along then, and tell Ralph I said hello."

After bidding her good-bye, he pulled out his cell phone and gave Ralph a call. They were able to make good progress before Millie called Ralph back to the restaurant.

By the time Matt returned to the store, the sun was about to set.

This time Grandma Rosella was awake and sitting at the table. "I'll wake her up," she said, standing. "She'll want to see you. I think she's had a rough time today."

Matt sat down at the kitchen table. He ought to have stayed in town with Coral instead of running off with Ralph this morning. He had every reason to think her trip to Tate's Hell might bother her. "I wish I'd hung around," he said. "I've texted her twice today but haven't heard a peep from her."

"Don't you worry, honey," Grandma Rosella said. "It's all right. She's just catching up on some rest."

What concerned him was the skull they found. If any of these ladies even suspected such a thing existed, it would distress them, Coral especially. And he hoped Coral hadn't figured it out, and it wasn't the cause of her long nap.

A bleary-eyed Coral appeared at the door of her bedroom. She smiled and smoothed her long wavy hair. "Hi, Matt," she said, and came on into the kitchen.

He rose and leaned forward to give her a kiss, but the sadness under her smile gave him pause.

"Are you okay?" he asked and took her by the hand. "I texted you twice."

After such a miserable day, I was so relieved to see my sweet Matt.

Out on Grandma Allie's back steps, he wrapped an arm around me and pulled me close. Sawdust clung to his tee shirt. While I napped, he and my dad had returned from Tallahassee and spent some quality time cutting up the log with newer and bigger borrowed equipment. The limbs were already gone, and now they'd sliced the main log horizontally like sections of a banana.

"I'm sorry, Coral," Matt said. "I know you had a rough day."

"Oh, Matt, you wouldn't believe it," I said and decided to leave out the part about Delia because I had no idea what was going on there. I told him all about our experience at Tate's Hell and then wrapped my arms around myself and leaned against him. "I never want to see that place again."

"Did you find anything special to keep—like a souvenir?"

I shook my head. "There was a broken bowl. Jessica and Dad saw it, and then the rain came and drove us out. They mentioned it was ugly and not worth saving, but I didn't care. It could stay right there in the dirt where they found it. Anything from that place would give me the creeps."

He gave my shoulders a squeeze. "What about the coin you found in the shell, does that give you the creeps?"

"Oh, wait," I said, standing. "You haven't even seen it yet, have you?"

"The famous gold piece? Ralph told me about it. I thought you'd never ask."

It only took a minute to run and get the shell with its little treasure inside. I emptied it into his hand to admire. He turned it over and over, studying the Indian head on the front and eagle on the back.

"Ten dollars," he said, chuckling at the wording on its front side. "I wonder how many more times than that it's really worth."

"No telling these days," I said.

He handed it back. "Do you have a box for it?"

I shrugged. "So far, I've been keeping it in this shell the way I found it. But I should look for a box."

We sat there in the quiet as darkness fell, and crickets began to sing. A distant hum of voices and laughter drifted over from the marina on the opposite side of the road. A salty fog began to descend. There was no greater feeling than sitting there beside the man I loved.

After a while he broke the silence. "Would you let me find you a box? And see what I can learn about the coin?"

I placed it in his hand. "Where would you go?"

"We passed a place up in Tallahassee…" He stood and set the coin and shell up on the post. "Say, you didn't answer my question." He pulled me up and close to him.

"What's that?"

He wrapped his arms around me. "Does the coin give you the creeps?"

I smiled and told him no. "The coin and the shells, they were Mama's."

He tipped my chin up and kissed me. "I'm glad to see that smile again. It bothers me when you're sad."

"I'm never sad—not when you're around."

On his way back to the cabin, Matt checked his phone again for any missed calls from his dad.

Once again, nothing.

Then he dialed Dad's number. Straight to voicemail. Was the battery dead? Was the phone off? There was no way to know.

He slid the phone into his pocket and gazed into the darkness.

Dad was an adult. He could find his way.

Though Matt didn't want to be a worrywart, maybe it was time to give Peter a call. And see what he had to say.

28

A late-morning rain poured into Sol's cupped hands, and he gulped it in until he was satisfied.

As the cloud passed over leaving gray skies, Sol wondered which direction was which. He guessed he was going the right way. He hoped so. Thinking back, though, when he left Las Vegas—which seemed like years ago—that method of navigating hadn't served him very well. When he sensed he was going east, he ended up west—in California.

This time, though, he was sure he was going the right way. So, he kept on weaving through the palmetto trails with a long stick across his shoulder and his pants and underwear dangling off the other end.

The problem was, though, even if he came across the road right now, he couldn't very well hitchhike.

With or without his pants, nobody would pick him up stinking like he did.

So, Sol trudged on from one small clearing to the next, hoping to find a sizeable water hole so he could wash his clothes, heavier now from all the rain, but just as stinky.

Then, late in the afternoon, he came across a large oak tree, the kind seen in front of southern mansions, with limbs swooping to the ground and draped everywhere. And just beyond it sparkled a fine clear pond about the size of a basketball court. Could have been a mudpuddle, Sol couldn't tell, but it was just perfect.

He took off his shirt and flip flops, dumped his dirty clothes into the shallow water nearby, and edged out to where it was a couple of feet deep. And there he lay down in the sun-warmed water to wash and float and relish its comfort. "Whooooo! Thank You, God!" he hollered into the sky.

Eventually, he returned to the shore where he snatched up his drifting clothes to give them a good scrubbing with sand and water. He got them fairly decent, though they were stained. At least they didn't stink.

He squeezed them out, spread the pants and undershorts across a bush to dry, and then scrubbed the shirt. He gave it a couple of final squeezes and tossed it over a bush. At the same time, he just happened to glance across the water again to admire the way the sun glimmered across it like yellow diamonds.

And that's when he noticed the log in the water that wasn't there before—not too far away—and floating in his direction—with two eyes. The realization hit, and he began to back away. A gator.

He'd heard these things were fast.

Then, as naked as a pig, he turned and made a beeline for that low-hanging limb—and climbed right up, hands and feet, hoping all the while that gators couldn't climb.

Panting but safe now at the top of the limb, Sol couldn't care less about his skinned-up knees and chest. He edged closer to the trunk and climbed another limb higher. Just in case the thing below decided it could do the same. One never knew about these wild creatures and what they could do. Heck, on the TV, Sol had even seen dogs climb trees.

The gator now lay glistening and wet up under the tree where it had surged out of the water behind him and missed.

Sol knew that if he did fall out of the tree, he'd be snapped up in those jaws. Reptile food.

He swallowed hard and stared down at the ugly creature. Had to be twelve-feet long. He wondered how many others were out there in the water.

Las Vegas didn't have gators. Not that he knew of, anyway. But Sol had watched shows in the past like that guy in Australia, or those dudes in Louisiana who hunted gators for fun. And he should have remembered, especially here in Florida, to be on the lookout for them.

And now his naked beat-up body would probably have to spend the whole night up in the tree—awake—to keep from falling out—because if Sol remembered right, nighttime is the time gators hunt their prey.

The sun rose over Sol's pond and sparkled like gems through the tree limbs below. He clawed anew at the welts on his arms, legs, and back side—and now knew for a fact that bugs lived up in the trees. Ants and roaches and other things had crawled over him in the night, and he'd spent the whole time wide awake flicking them off. He could hardly wait to get away.

The gator was long gone now, but Sol hadn't taken any chances with its feeding times. After sun-up, he'd waited a good long time before descending.

In spite of spending the whole night in a tree with no sleep, he still felt better than yesterday. Must have been all the water he'd drunk from the pond yesterday.

Hydration. And now he needed more.

Without the gator's interference.

"Thank You, God," he whispered in case the gator was listening and climbed down into the weeds.

To the right, Sol's clothes remained draped across the bushes. He tiptoed down to the water's edge where he glanced around, knelt, and cupped his hands. Then he drank until his stomach could hold no more. With his belly sloshing, he tiptoed back and snagged his clothes off the bushes.

After he pulled them back on, he paused, his ears alert. Was that a...?

Yes, a siren! Its wail grew louder and louder until maybe a hundred yards to the left of his oak it howled its loudest and then moved away into the distance.

"Thank You, God!" he yelled as loud as he could and raised both arms. He gave them a pump. That's all he needed to find his way to the road.

Come to think of it, his head didn't throb at all now.

Over where the siren sounded its loudest, he marked a tree and made a crooked beeline for it through the maze of palmettos.

Come hell or high water, he was about to get out of this place.

29

At the restaurant, Ralph slid a plate through the order window. Millie, with a downcast face, reached in to pick it up.

"Don't be mad, Millie." He spoke softly—sweetly even—in hopes she'd get over the fact that Delia Blue-Hair was working tonight in the other dining room. Millie, who now brushed past her without a word, barely tolerated the sight of the girl.

Ralph's other part-time waitress had already quit because of Delia, letting them know she'd be back when Delia left, and now Millie was filling both spots. Things were going south fast for Ralph.

If only he could fix things.

He paused for a brief second while a bolt of wisdom lit up in his brain. *Well, why not? Why wait?*

So, as she walked away, he darted into the back room and reached over the washer for the two neatly packaged gifts. He'd wrapped them himself. Pink paper and lavender bows from Dollar General. She'd like that.

Tucking them under his arm, he scurried back to the window before she returned.

But instead of Millie, Delia pranced up and laid her arms up on the ledge as he approached. He hated to think what the customers could see of her from the dining room and hoped at least the lunch bar blocked the view. If only he had a wrap-around apron for her.

Delia spotted the gifts. "What's that in your arms, Ralphie?"

He ignored the question, bumped the gifts up under the window frame where she couldn't see them, and topped off her waiting plates with dill pickles. Up on the ledge, he nudged the dishes against her elbows and gave her the coldest glare he could muster. "Call me Ralph, or Mr. Ralph, or nothing at all."

Hardly flustered, she took the plates, glanced back over her shoulder, and batted her eyes. She headed back to her dining room.

Ralph snorted.

Millie turned away from her table and approached, a new ticket in her hand. She placed it on a clip. Ralph touched his finger to his lips and leaned forward. "Hey," he whispered.

That caught her attention. Nobody whispered around here. She paused to meet his glance. "Hey," she whispered back. "What's up?"

"Remember that broken coffee cup? The red one?"

"Whaaa…?" She wrinkled her nose. "You wanna talk about that now? In the middle of work?"

He grinned and silently placed the gifts in front of her.

Her mouth flew open, "Oh!"

"Open them up," he said and made sure she had the box he'd marked with a 1 in front of her first. "It'll break, so be careful."

"Oh, Ralph," she said, as she slipped off the wrappings and opened the box. She glanced over her shoulder toward the dining room. "My customers…"

"Here, let me help you pull it out." For now, he had to keep her from seeing the gold letters on the cup.

She lifted it, running her fingertips over the gilt edges and the matching saucer. "It's beautiful," she cooed as he guided the cup and saucer down to the window ledge. He turned the cup upside down on the dish with the foam padding under it.

"Why are you doing that?"

"I don't want it to tip over. You've got another gift to open."

In the meantime, Delia approached, saw the gifts, and opened her mouth to interfere. Ralph was having none of it. He stopped the girl with an outstretched finger and waved it in a circle in the direction of the dining room, a clear order to go refresh the drinks.

Delia whirled around and left, properly scolded.

By now Millie had the other gift unwrapped, and out of the box. "A matching pair," she cooed, turning the first one around. "What's thi—"

The fancy gold letters were hidden behind the packaging.

"Wait, not yet," Ralph said, and directed her to the second cup, its rim barely at eye level with her. "Look down inside there," he said, removing a thin piece of wadded foam. He tipped the cup.

"What's this little white box?"

She leaned away as she gazed at Ralph and then reached for the box and pulled off its white lid. She peeked inside. "A black velvet jewelry box?" A look of pleasure and disbelief crossed her face. "What have you gone and done, Ralph? What have you—"

Her hands shook as she pried up its hinged lid. She gasped and stared, her hand over her mouth. Tears filled her eyes.

"Will you have me, Millie? Will you marry me, please?"

Tears dropped onto her wrist as she gazed from him to the sparkling diamonds and back again. "Oh, yes, yes, yes, Ralph." She held up the box, letting the gems sparkle in the kitchen's light. "It's beautiful, just beauuuutiful!"

He'd bought her the fanciest ring he could find.

"Here, let me help you put it on," he said, taking it from the box and fitting it onto her trembling finger. He knew her size from one of her other rings.

"Ohhh! Ohhh!" seemed to be the limit of her vocabulary.

"Did you see the letters on the cups?" he said and removed the rest of the padding. He turned the cups to face her, *Husband* and *Wife.*

"Oh, Ralph," she said, and clasped a hand against her heart. "I have no words. I thought you'd never ask. Lean over here and let me kiss you, honey. I'm glad I broke that old red cup. I should have done that a long, long time ago."

She reached for his face, and as they leaned toward each other, the dining room erupted in applause and whistles.

"I'm glad you did, too." He kissed her again.

After his phone conversation with Fine China, Glitter, and Gems in Tallahassee, Matt said good-bye and gazed down at the items scattered over his sunlit cotton bedspread. Among them lay a little white box he'd scrounged up from Millie and stacks of bills in varying denominations—his savings from Zeke and everything he brought with him to Carrabelle.

He'd run his plans by Grandma Rosella who was thrilled with it all. Plenty able, she'd offered to help, but he'd refused. Some things a man had to do for himself.

Matt lifted off the box's lid and unfolded the protective tissue around Coral's coin, examining it once again. Then he packed it all back and shoved the box into his pants pocket. He couldn't help but smile. Coral was going to like his surprise.

He patted the box through his pocket and then stacked the cash and stuffed it into his wallet. Jewelry stores weren't cheap. And he may not have much left after this, but it didn't matter. He was standing on his own two feet.

Since Zeke's charter business was on hold for the time being, Matt's income had dropped like a rock off a cliff.

And if the price the man gave him on the phone was right, he'd soon be seeking additional employment.

As much as he hated it, Matt might have to give in to Ralph's request and go work at the restaurant.

Being a waiter was going to be as bad as a trip to the dentist.

It wasn't the work that bothered him, he could learn anything.

It was that girl.

But didn't Ralph say he was working on that?

As long as she stayed in her dining room, he would stay in his.

30

Matt decided to drive the Mustang this morning and pick up Coral at Aunt Allie's instead of them walking to the beach. He didn't have a lot of time, and he wanted to take her to breakfast before going to the lighthouse.

He pulled into the restaurant parking lot with her, parked, and turned off the ignition. He needed to explain to Coral about Ralph needing his help at the restaurant.

As he walked her in, and before they reached the front door, he paused. Might as well get it over with.

"I know you've noticed that my work with Zeke is falling off." Coral knew all the reasons. "And his old deck hand is healing up."

She gazed up at him with those beautiful blue eyes. "So, what are you trying to tell me?"

He grimaced. "Your dad asked me to help him."

Coral gave him a long look. "Like what *kind* of help? In the restaurant? I thought you refused to do that."

Matt heaved a sigh. "He's begging me."

"Matt, I'm not going to tell you what to do. What do you want to do?"

He pushed open the door and whispered as they stepped in. "He's your dad, Coral. How can I tell him no?"

Millie, wearing an unusually broad smile, welcomed them in. "Just take a seat, kids. I'll bring you some coffee."

"Wow, she's in a good mood," Matt said.

They sat in their favorite spot near the door, and before they could study the menus, Millie returned with coffees and placed them on the table. "Oh, y'all, have I got some news for you," she said, still grinning. "But hang on a second, because I've got to go get Ralph first," she said across her shoulder as she practically danced through the kitchen door.

"Must be something very good," Coral said, smiling. But her expression faded when the blue-haired waitress appeared and rested her hip against their table. Her back side was practically in Coral's face.

Coral leaned away.

"Hi, there, handsome," she cooed. "It's good to see you again." She pulled out her pad and pen and maintained her pose as if Coral weren't even present. "What can I get you?"

Millie and Ralph stepped out of nowhere and stood behind the girl. Millie tapped her on the shoulder.

Delia turned toward her with a smirk, and Millie pointed toward the other room. "That's your dining room in there, Delia."

Delia shoved her pad into her apron pocket and pranced away, clearly displeased.

Ralph crossed his arms and watched her leave.

Millie dusted her hands together. "Little twit." But then she turned back to Matt and Coral with a fresh smile. "Well. Guess what, kids. We've got an announcement." She stuck out her hand with the glittering engagement ring and rocked it back and forth.

Coral pressed her hand against her mouth. "You're engaged? That is so gorgeous!"

"Millie said yes," Ralph blurted out. "She said yes!"

Coral jumped up and gave her a big squeeze. "Oh, ya'll, I'm so happy for you! Congratulations." She turned to Ralph and gave him one too. "This is great news, Dad. Congratulations."

Matt, on his feet now, shook Ralph's hand. "Good job, man, I'm happy for you." He gave Millie a hug. "Who else knows?"

"Not a soul," Millie said, whispering now. "But we want to tell them ourselves, okay?"

Matt nodded and zipped his lips. "We'll leave that to you, then."

They chatted for a minute, with Ralph and Millie relaying the story about the proposal. More customers filtered in, and Ralph said, "Well, kids, we've got to get back to work."

Millie took their orders for pancakes and eggs and headed back to the kitchen.

As they waited on their order, Coral spoke first. "Matt, I know you're trying to do the right thing working and all…"

"And yes, I know you're concerned about that blue-haired girl. But don't be." He took her hand and looked into her face. "I only have eyes for you."

"What are you going to do about her? She's all over you. It's sickening."

He lowered his voice to a whisper. "She's on her way out. Ralph's getting rid of her."

"But what about for the time being?"

"She's got her own dining room—in there," Matt said. "I don't think…"

"Just be careful. She's bad news."

He nodded. "It's just for a short time. A very short time. And anyway, did you see Millie correct her just now? Mother hen."

Coral smiled, and he let the conversation rest, but he could tell Coral wasn't too keen on the idea. He didn't blame her.

Matt and I rode down to the Crooked River Lighthouse where a canopy of tall pines shaded the well-kept museum. Along this southern gulf coast, the pines and palmettos were just as common as the palms and hammocks of other parts of Florida. "I've been looking forward to this," I said.

He gave me a wink and reached for my hand. "I want to spend every minute I can with you."

The lighthouse and museum weren't but a little way past the beach entrance and overlooked a wide stretch of the beautiful Gulf of Mexico. We parked under the pines and strolled across the freshly mowed lawn to climb the steps.

But as we reached the door, Matt's phone rang. He checked his screen. "It's Mom," he mouthed, followed by a "sorry" as he motioned me back toward the top step where we took a seat.

I only heard one end of the conversation.

"Hi, Mom."

His mother's voice came through, but I couldn't make out the words as she spoke her brief couple of sentences.

"You're what?" Matt's expression showed surprise, disbelief. "Today?" He rubbed his forehead. "So, like, why? Why are you coming to Carrabelle?"

He waited in silence while his mother said something.

"You want to see Dad. Okaaay. I get that. And to see me. Okay." He looked at me with raised eyebrows. "Yes, I haven't spoken to him, but I know he's on the way."

I guessed Matt was talking about his dad.

He listened for a long moment, then, "Mom. Stop a minute. Hold on. And listen to me. What brought this on, I mean, why are you coming here to connect with Dad? What changed?"

I studied my nails while a series of cars passed between us and the beach and wondered what was going on.

"Okay, then," Matt finally said. "I'll see you at two o'clock. Tallahassee International Airport. And what airline?" He sighed. "I love you too."

After he hung up, he turned to me. "I guess you figured out what was going on, right?"

"She's coming in expecting to see your dad?"

"With Eddie. He's an employee about our age, nice guy, something about a car. Anyway, I already have to drive up to Tallahassee today, and the airport's on the same side of town."

"One thing I'm curious about. You asked her what's changed."

"Yeah. Get this. She said something's happened to Dad. He's changed. She sounded kind of excited."

On the way to pick up his mother at the airport, Matt stopped off at Fine China, Glitter, and Gems. The salesman was with another customer, and Matt had time to, once again, examine the jewelry-laden glass cases.

Eventually, the other customer left, and Matt was glad to have the salesman's undivided attention.

Matt had several questions as he set the white box on top of the counter. As expected, the salesman answered them all.

"You say you'll be driving up to the airport?" the man said as he took the gold coin out of Matt's box. "I should be able to have this ready for you within an hour."

"That's perfect," Matt said. "I should be back by then."

31

After lunch, I stepped out onto the back porch. Grandma Allie came out and joined me. She leaned her cane up against the rock post, and there we sat for a while, rocking and gazing across the small bit of highway we could see and listening to the gulls over at the marina.

Matt was off at the airport, and Jessica and Grandma Rosella were in Tallahassee visiting Jessica's mom.

We could have taken a drive, but I had no vehicle.

"I sure miss everyone," I said.

"It's lonely, yes," Grandma Allie said. "But when a person lives as long as I have, they learn to tolerate it."

Properly rebuked, I regretted my comment. How many years had she spent alone? "I'm sorry, Grandma. I didn't mean to complain. I'm just used to all the happy voices."

She waved away my comment. "Oh, I knew what you meant. And I miss them, too. But these days with Rosella and all you young'uns coming in and out and Ralph back in my life, I'm not really lonely. Sure, they're gone for the day, but they'll be back. You don't know what a blessing you all are."

But I wasn't about to sit here all day rocking. I lowered my hands to the armrests. "Well, since it's just us," I stood, "what kind of trouble can we get into?" She wasn't used to getting out and doing anything, but maybe there was something…

I gave her some space to consider it.

After a bit, she said, "How about the library? Now that I've got my glasses fixed—you know how Rosella always has a book in her hand—I'd like to find something more interesting than large-print *Reader's Digests*."

"You want to walk over to the library?"

At the bottom of the steps, Grandma Allie gripped my elbow, and we strolled the one-and-a-half blocks to the library. The Carrabelle Library was a nice modern building with lots of glass. Its ice-cold air conditioning sank over us as we entered.

"Good thing you brought that sweater, isn't it?" I teased. Her beloved gray sweater, threadbare in places, went everywhere she went. And today was no exception. Yet she didn't make a move to put it on.

For the most part, she disliked air conditioning. Her store had none, but because of its high ceilings and good ventilation, one hardly noticed. The few times I'd walked her over to the grocery store, she complained about its chill. For now, though, she was focused on the facility.

"Ohh, this is nice," she whispered, admiring all the books. "You know, this new building was a long time coming. I haven't been to the library since it resided in the music room of the old Carrabelle school."

"It is nice," I agreed, and made a mental note to scope out the old one.

She sighed. "I really should get out more." Then she wandered toward the shelves.

"You go ahead," I said. "I'll be in here." I doubled back to explore a room near the entrance marked Friends of the Library. I was used to shopping in such places where the used-book prices were a bargain. Grandma Rosella and I spent many happy hours in the one down at Ft. Myers.

I stepped inside, and there, partly hidden behind the cash register and several piles of books, stood a very old man with wire spectacles. His pleasant voice carried a tremble of frailty. "Morning, young lady."

His volunteer tag read *Jessie S, Retired* and under that *Justice of the Peace* and several gold stars. In his hand was a sheet of pre-printed price tags, and he was busy sticking them onto the book bindings.

"Morning, sir. Beautiful library you have here."

"You from out of town?"

"Ft. Myers," I said.

"Then welcome. You came at the perfect time. We've got a bunch of new titles on the shelves."

With a nod and a thank you, I wandered down the first aisle. Time seemed to disappear as I perused the titles and categories and great prices. When I glanced up at the clock, twenty minutes had passed.

And there in the doorway stood Grandma Allie, in her sweater. "Are you ready to go?" she whispered.

"Absolutely," I said, knowing I could come back any time I liked. No need to tire her out. "Did you find something?"

"Sure did." She held up two books and a library card. "I'm all set. Now what did you find?"

"We've got to get Jessica down here," I said. "She'd been looking for cookbooks and they've got a huge selection back there."

I waved good-bye to the little man. "See you later, Mr. Jessie."

32

Tall pines flickered by the windows as Jessica steered north toward Tallahassee with Grandma Rosella next to her. The elderly lady and her family had quickly become as close as family.

When Jessica mentioned today's trip to Tallahassee to visit her mom, Grandma asked if she could tag along.

Today would be Miss Rosella's second trip to the city, and Jessica was proud of her favorite patient for growing so strong.

But still, she hesitated. Grandma Rosella was such a—a lady, and Jessica's mother was a total character.

"When you meet Mama—I mean—I hope you won't think bad …" she began.

Grandma gave Jessica's arm a reassuring pat. "Nothing bothers me, honey. I've seen it all."

Jessica let out her breath. It helped to know Grandma had once worked the casinos out in Las Vegas.

"Thank you. And thanks for understanding. Mama's going to love meeting you."

It wasn't clear what Grandma Rosella had in mind by tagging along today. But that wasn't a worry.

When Jessica and Coral became friends, Coral shared how Grandma Rosella had influenced her life—no—saved it when Coral's mom moved them into that broken-down trailer and subjected Coral to her male traffic. Their neighbor Rosella realized Coral's danger and stepped in, eventually taking her in. It changed everything for Coral. The tiny woman, though, was no more Coral's real grandma than she was Jessica's. And now Jessica loved her too. Rosella, with those halo-like braids on top of her head, and her spunky Hawaiian florals, always seemed to know what to say or do.

"I can't say I have a special agenda today," Grandma said, as if she could read Jessica's thoughts. "Other than to keep you company. But now that Coral's found her father, I know that you've been worrying about finding your own."

"I'm not trying to be envious. I just want to know who he is."

"God's Word says he sets the solitary in families. Did you notice He's been doing that for you?"

Jessica gave her a quick glance that evolved into a smile. "Of course. You—and Coral, she's like a sister—and—and well, all of you."

Grandma patted her arm.

"But I do have an agenda," Jessica said. "Only one thing, every time I come here. I want to prod Mama again and get her to tell me who my father is. Dead or alive, at least I'd have his name. I don't even want to dig into his history—not after the awful things Coral discovered about her own family tree."

"I see."

She turned to Rosella. "I just want a name."

Rosella gave her another pat. "You may not want to hear this, but keep it in mind. God knows best. Maybe it's not in your best interest to know who the man is."

Jessica heaved a sigh. Grandma was right, although she didn't want to hear that. But it was a possibility.

"Don't worry. We'll pray. Let's ask God to lead and guide us with His Holy Spirit today."

Jessica nodded and focused on the road as Grandma said a quick prayer.

Buildings and shops condensed as they drove into the city. Before long, they turned down the familiar gravel lane leading up to Jessica's mother's old but respectable mobile home park. As they swung left, her mother's small trailer appeared at the far end. Its full-length sunporch, mostly an array of open jalousie windows, revealed its tidy interior, an arrangement of rattan furniture with green and white pillows.

As Jessica parked the car and stepped out, Mom's parrot belted out its familiar squawks, "Fine as a frog's hair," it said, and tacked on a couple of cuss-words Mama used on the phone. Jessica grinned.

Grandma Rosella, her feet already on the gravel, laughed. "Nothing like a happy hello, right?" she said, putting Jessica at ease. "Gorgeous bird."

The colorful creature perched between her mother's potted palms. Behind him gaped the trailer's front door, and down its metal steps bounded a barking little Yorkie who danced on its back legs and further welcomed them.

"Mom, we're here," Jessica called out, as if Mama couldn't already tell.

Jessica circled the car and reached into the backseat for Grandma's walker. "Oh, that dog. He is one spoiled pet, let me tell you. All her animals are. She takes him everywhere."

With Grandma steadied on her walker, Jessica reached into the backseat for the bag of shells she and Coral had collected, a gift for Jessica's mom who loved such things.

And now a well-made-up blonde of around fifty floated down the steps and burst through the side jalousie door.

Jessica had told Mama she was bringing a guest, and now the woman's raspy smoker's voice welcomed them. "Oh, Jessica, baby, it's so good to see you." She opened her arms, extending the width of her colorful muumuu like wings as she hugged Jessica and then Grandma. She leaned back and directed her smiling approval at the older lady. "Well, this is the wonderful Grandma Rosella you told me about. So happy to meet you, honey. Welcome." She gave Rosella a second hug.

Jessica's mom, slightly hard of hearing and fairly loud, was younger than Grandma Rosella, but no matter. Everybody was honey to her.

"This is my mother, Lara," Jessica said.

"So pleased to meet you too, Lara," Rosella said.

They followed Lara around to the other side of the porch where Jessica gathered up the bouncing Yorkie.

He squirmed and wiggled to lick Jessica's face, and she turned away. "Settle down, Squirt. Settle down."

"Settle down, Squirt. Settle down," the bird repeated as they stepped into the ground-level porch.

Lara calmed the pets and doled out their treats as the visitors seated themselves on the palm-frond prints.

"Lovely place you have," Grandma told her. "I'm partial to tropical motifs and bright colors myself."

"Well, thank you so much," Lara said. Rings glittered on her fingers as she reached for the lighter and cigarettes on the table and offered Rosella a smoke.

Rosella smiled and shook her head, but it didn't stop Lara from lighting up.

"Now I'm eager to hear all the news from down at the coast," Lara said as smoke rose and disappeared under the ceiling fan. "It's always good to see my Jessica come home. I'm so proud of her."

The conversation kickstarted around Jessica's nursing adventures and led into reports of Grandma's progression from sickness. "She's so much better, now," Jessica said. "This is her second trip to Tallahassee. And wait till you hear about Coral, Aunt Allie, Matt, and all my other new friends."

"Yeah, I'm certainly glad you ditched that old boyfriend."

Jessica ignored the comment. She hadn't come here to talk about that subject. She reached for the bag of shells. "My friend Coral and I picked these up for you at the beach." She opened the brown bag.

Her mom peeked inside. "Oooh, so pretty! But where are my manners?" Mama said, taking the bag. "Would you all like some iced tea and cookies? They aren't homemade, just regular old store-bought ones."

Jessica jumped up. "I'll get them, Mama. You go ahead and look at the shells."

"Thank you, honey. You know where everything is. Just shoo those cats off the counter if they get in your way."

As Jessica stepped inside, she peeked back around the doorframe to find her mother dumping the shells onto her lap and admiring them. She turned each one over with her freshly manicured fingertips. "Oh, aren't these lovely?" she asked Rosella. "I think I'll make a wind chime with them. See?" She pointed out the end of a shell.

"I can drill holes right here and string them up there in the corner." Her mom's mega-volume carried into the kitchen.

Jessica smiled.

Her mother's conversation turned back to Rosella. "I'm so happy my Jessica's got nice friends. I worry sometimes. You know?"

"I do," Rosella said. "And maybe someday you can come down for a visit and meet the whole gang. We'd love to have you."

"Oh, I don't know about that, now."

For some reason, Jessica's mom never wanted to go south to the Gulf.

Before long, Jessica was back with the cookies and tea on a tray.

The conversation continued with hardly a pause, with tales of fishing boats, sharks, and injuries. Jessica's mother shared her own news, mostly of work at the grocery where she cashiered, and before Jessica realized it, more than an hour had passed. "Mama, this has been great. But we need to get Grandma Rosella back so she can maintain her rest."

Lara nodded as they stood. "You just come back as often as you can, honey. I miss you. And you too, Miss Rosella. It was a lovely visit. Come back anytime."

"Before we go, Mama…" Jessica turned to Rosella and held up a finger for her to hang on a minute. She put one arm around her mother and turned toward the door. Then she lowered her voice. "Mama, I ask you every time and you brush me off. Can't you just tell me? Tell me my father's name."

"No, you don't want to know that, Jessica, now *shhh*! Please quit asking me. I don't want to talk about it."

Jessica sighed and looked up at the ceiling, tears in her eyes. She hugged her mama. "One day you're going to have to tell me. Just don't wait until it's too late. I only want a name. I'm not planning on looking him up or getting ya'll back together."

Lara choked up too. She kissed her daughter's cheek and swatted her behind. "You go on out to the car, now, and I'll walk Miss Rosella out behind you."

Jessica headed toward the car. But her mother, oblivious to the meaning of whisper, turned back to Rosella. "To tell you the truth…" she mumbled.

Jessica slowed and inclined her ear.

"Rosella, I have no idea who her…" But the last words faded into the racket of a revving engine down the street.

Jessica's jaw dropped as she opened the driver's side door and climbed in. She sat there in stunned silence. After all this time, had Mama said what Jessica thought she had? To someone she just met?

In the meantime, her mother opened the passenger door, slid the walker into the backseat for Grandma, and helped her in. She slammed her door as if nothing special had occurred and backed away to wave and blow kisses at Jessica as she started the engine.

The sting of her mother's words raced through Jessica's bloodstream. She put the car in reverse and pressed the accelerator, trying to keep from stomping it.

At the stop sign, Jessica turned to Grandma. She gazed into her eyes, her heart thrumming for all it was worth. "What did Mama tell you back there?"

"What do you think you heard?"

Jessica winced and took a deep breath as she turned onto the next street. Such evasiveness. But then, Grandma wouldn't betray a confidence.

Tears burned behind Jessica's lids. She turned to Grandma. "Mama doesn't know, does she? She doesn't even know who he is."

Grandma sighed and rested her hand on Jessica's shoulder.

33

At the airport, Matt located his mother, Paulette, and Eddie at the front pick-up area. Her red hair fell in waves around her shoulders, just like the old days, and her emerald eyes shone as pretty as ever. When she recognized him behind the wheel of the Mustang, she clapped her hands and waved with excitement as if everything was beautiful in the whole wide world and she'd never deserted him and his dad at all.

He had forgiven her, hadn't he? He returned the warm greeting with a smile and searched for a spot where he could parallel park, while hoping she didn't dash out and get herself run over.

Eddie stood calmly beside her and lifted his own hand in greeting. Matt parked and climbed out with a chuckle, imagining Eddie's embarrassment at having to stand next to this hyperactive lady.

He circled the car and wrapped his mom in a warm hug, receiving more than he gave as she latched on and swung him back and forth.

"That's good, Mom. That's good," he protested.

"Oh, honey, I'm just so… It's so good to see you." She leaned away and pinched his cheeks. "Ohhh, son. What a handsome man you've become. A sight to behold."

He noticed what seemed to be genuine tears in her eyes. "You, too, Mom. It's good to see you."

He hoped her efforts to meet up with Dad didn't build up to a disappointing climax with her discovering he hadn't changed at all and then backing out of the picture again for another four years. For the time being, Matt would just go along with things and not get his hopes up.

He'd come to his own conclusions after he saw Dad. And that should be pretty soon.

Once again he checked his phone. No missed calls.

Matt combed through the details and couldn't come up with any reason why Dad would stop off or delay his coming up here.

As Matt rolled out of the airport, his mother spoke up from the passenger seat. Long-legged Eddie, with his knees sideways, was crammed in the back. "Honey, I want you to stop somewhere so I can treat you boys to lunch."

Mom and Eddie had had some layovers between Las Vegas and Tallahassee. "I'm sorry, Mom, I didn't even think about you all being hungry."

He was glad she wanted to treat, though, because he sure didn't have the money to pay for three meals and the jeweler. A delay would also kill some time before he was due back at the store.

"Thanks, Mom. There is a nice little buffet that's not too far."

"Sure. That's fine," she said. "I'm not particular. You know, in the old days, they served a meal on every flight."

"I'll take care of my own meal, no worries," Eddie said, trying to be helpful.

"No, you won't, honey," Paulette retorted, twisting around toward the back seat. "While we're on this trip, you're my son too."

Eddie had traveled along to gather his vehicle from Sol. "I appreciate that, ma'am."

"But," she added, "make sure to contact your mom in Las Vegas and let her know you arrived safe and sound."

Matt tried to catch Eddie's expression in the rear-view mirror, but the suitcases blocked his view. They were mostly Mom's, with two smaller ones in the trunk. Eddie, with his back pressed up against the left window, was just out of range.

A half mile down the road, they arrived at the Bounteous Buffet, where the selections were thin and the midafternoon crowd even thinner. "Good timing," Matt said as they filed in past the register to the buffet line.

At the table, Matt bowed his head as usual, accustomed to blessing his food. But Mom interrupted. "Honey, would you let me bless our food?" She took Eddie by one hand and Matt by the other. Neither she nor Dad had ever prayed over their meals.

It took a second for this to register. "Of course, Mom."

"Dear Lord, we thank You for this delightful abundance. Bless the food and sanctify it, and bless our trip, and bless Matt in his budding romance. In Jesus' name, Amen."

"Amen," Matt said, and Eddie followed suit.

Matt took up his fork and considered this new development.

Dad couldn't be the only one who'd changed.

And now he had to ask. "Mom, you told me Dad was different. Would this be a good time to tell me about it?"

After Matt's question, his mom took a bite of her macaroni salad and glanced across the table at Eddie as she gave it some thought. She swallowed and pointed her fork at Eddie. "Eddie's going to have to help me answer that, Matt. It's a bit of a story."

"Well, go ahead. And I hope you're right, Mom. I really do. It's something I've been hoping for my whole life." Matt still wasn't going to get his hopes up.

"She's right," Eddie said. "It's a story."

"To start off with, your dad borrowed Eddie's car. For the trip down here," Mom said.

Yep, Dad was scared to death of flying.

"And he left his Mercedes locked up in the garage—after telling Eddie he could borrow it while he was gone."

"Okay. Nothing new there."

"So, in the meantime, I've been doing a little change-around myself, wanting to say my prayers, read the Bible, and get serious about what comes next in my life. I realized I need to see if maybe your dad and I can patch things up. Like make things right," Mom said, "even though I know he's flawed. Severely. I thought maybe we should backtrack—retrace our steps and get married like we should have done in the beginning before I had you. You know what I mean?"

Matt nodded—the second thing he'd wished for all his life.

"So," she held up her hands, "I was just trying to get things right in my life."

Matt put his hand on her shoulder. "That's good, Mom. Real good. And then?"

"So—so then, I came back to town only to find out about his trip down here. And Eddie's car."

"And she was mad," Eddie said. "Real mad when she found out about the car and how he tricked me."

"So Matt, there I was, just trying to figure out what to do, whether to forget the whole thing or what."

"Your mom got the car out of his garage and told me to go ahead and drive it," Eddie said. "She made sure I had wheels. I was stuck, man, me and my mom, without a car."

Eddie's mom was a single parent in poor health. And he was her main support.

"First off, I needed to help Eddie. He couldn't run the shop all by himself, day after day," she said. "I took some of the hours off his shoulders."

"And then," Eddie said, "she saw the credit card statement."

"Credit card statement?" Matt said.

"And there were the tires. Spanking new name-brand tires, bought somewhere, I can't remember, Arizona, Texas…"

"Couldn't have been for anything else but my car," Eddie said. "Mine were about bald, and ready to blow. I did try to warn him before he left, but he was so fixated on borrowing the car, he wouldn't even listen."

"Sounds like Dad."

"Nothing added up, Matt." She fluffed the back of her red hair. "I know your dad. If he bought anything, he most certainly would have bought retreads."

"How do you know he wasn't going to charge Eddie or take it out of his pay?"

"Your mom asked him," Eddie said. "She called him up and point blank asked him."

"Because Eddie was worried about it. He couldn't afford expensive tires. With his little paycheck he'd have put on retreads too."

"So Dad told you what?" Matt wanted to know.

"He said, 'Don't worry about it. It's a gift.' A *gift*, Matt. Since when has your dad ever done anything like that?"

Matt frowned. "Strange."

"And then the wreck," Eddie said.

Matt leaned back. "Dad had a wreck? Was he hurt?"

His mom reached out her hand. "Not a bad one, just a run-in with a post."

"But," Eddie added, "it needed body work and paint. And you know how old my paint job is—was."

"So he calls me," Mom said, "and wants to know what color Eddie would like his car painted."

Matt leaned forward. "He wanted to know Eddie's preference?" That was new. Matt shook his head. "You're mistaken, right? You're sure he didn't mean something else?"

"Sounded like a whole paint job, honey."

"And then," Eddie said, pointing at Matt, "and then, there was the letter."

"Yes, the letter," Mom said. "And that completely blew my mind."

Matt crossed his arms and leaned back against the booth. This he had to hear.

Matt studied Mom as she reached into her purse. She pulled out a folded light blue paper.

"Here, Matt, take a look."

He unfolded the letter to find its printed baby design covered in a small, neat handwriting. *Dear Mr. Sol Flores*, it began.

"Read it out loud," his mother said, "I'd like to hear it again."

Matt leaned his wrists against the table and began, "Dear Mr. Sol Flores, My husband and I are deeply indebted to you for stopping on the highway to give us assistance with gas. Thanks to you, we made it to the hospital just in time to survive a very complicated and frightening delivery. To make a long story short, we want you to know how honored we were to name our beautiful baby boy after you, Solomon Fernando Rains. Sincerely, the Rains family. PS. My husband is keeping that red gas can as a remembrance of you and your kindness, but rest assured, we will pass on the kindness."

Matt turned to his mother. "Something has happened."

However, Matt would still hold off his final opinion until he saw his dad in person.

On the way to the car, following lunch with his mom and Eddie, Matt checked his phone again for missed calls from Dad.

Not one. *Shoot.*

Once again, he dialed Dad's number.

Straight to voicemail.

Maybe it was time to call Peter. But what could he report? Given the car's new paint job, Dad's unknown clothing and so on, if he was a missing person, Matt had very little to offer the investigators.

Grandma Allie and I returned from the library, and she went in to reopen the store. I took off to the grocery down the street for some hamburger meat for supper. After making my purchase, I stepped outside the store and call Jessica. By now, she should have been on her way back from Tallahassee with Grandma Rosella.

I was eager to hear how it went and to get her down to the library. She needed to see all those fantastic cookbooks. They'd be open until seven tonight.

But when she answered, she didn't sound like herself.

"Are you okay?" I asked.

"Not really," she said. "I'll bring Grandma home and call you afterward. I'll be helping Millie, so I can't stay."

In the company of Mom and Eddie, Matt stopped by the jewelry store and picked up Coral's surprise. Then he drove his mother and Eddie straight to Aunt Allie's back door and knocked on the door. Aunt Allie answered, and he introduced them. Coral wasn't there. She'd gone up to the grocery for a few items.

"I'm sorry, Aunt Allie, for not giving you a heads-up."

She waved it away, "Oh, pshaw. That's all right." She turned to the newcomers. "It's a pleasure to meet you, Paulette and Eddie," she said and pulled the screen door open wide. "Come on in, everyone." She patted Matt's arm as his mother passed by. "And this young fellow—you should be mighty proud of him—Matt is a wonderful young man."

"Oh, yes he is," Paulette gushed. She leaned in and gave him a kiss on the cheek as she passed by. "Yes, he certainly is."

"Step on through there," Aunt Allie said and followed them into the kitchen.

"This building where we stand," Matt said, drawing the attention away from himself, "is Aunt Allie's boarding house, more than a hundred years old." He pointed his thumb back toward the dining room, or *parlor,* as Aunt Allie sometimes called it. "And her store is through the door back there."

Eddie stood back as Paulette pivoted in a slow circle. "Oh, my goodness gracious, Mrs. Bentley, I am just stunned by your place," she said. "It is so historic, so original, so quaint, I…I just can't take it all in!"

"Just call me Aunt Allie. All my friends do."

Paulette nodded. "Well, then, Aunt Allie it is."

"I told them you rent rooms," Matt said. "Is there any way you would you be able…?"

Aunt Allie hesitated. "I would love to, Matt, and I've got three more rooms upstairs. But since Rosella and Coral and Jessica moved in, I've decided I'd better backtrack, save up some money and get the whole place rewired. I'd better not put more load on these old wires."

Paulette reached out her hand. "Oh, now don't you worry, Aunt Allie. Not one minute of it. We can stay at the bed and breakfast Matt told us about. It's perfectly fine. And here," she said, setting her purse on the table and reaching inside for her wallet. She flipped it open and pulled out a handful of bills without even looking at them. She laid it on Aunt Allie's table. "Let me be the first to donate to your cause."

Wiring? Matt gazed at the money in Aunt Allie's hand.

A cold chill ran through him. He'd never even considered how sketchy the wiring might be. Plunging his hand into his pocket, he found his wallet. He flipped it open and pulled out his last twenty. He placed it beside his mom's cash.

Eddie did the same.

Matt wished he had more.

Aunt Allie stared down at the cluttered bills. "I have to tell you folks, I'm ashamed to take your money. But I certainly can use it, and I do thank you. It's a mighty slow job saving money on a budget."

Her store was more of a hobby or landmark than an income.

"Aunt Allie," Matt said, "I had no idea. Why didn't you mention this?"

"It's a recent decision," she said.

They visited a few more minutes. Then Matt drove them to the bed and breakfast to get Mom and Eddie set up with rooms. "I'm sorry you didn't get to meet everyone else, but you will pretty soon," he said.

"That's all right, Matt. I'm sure Eddie wants to get cleaned up the same as I do and put on some fresh clothes."

After he departed, Matt thought back to the old store. He wondered why something as important as wiring hadn't crossed his mind. Now he had even more reason to work—and to pray for everyone's safety. He picked up his phone and called his friend/boss Zeke. "Got a minute?"

At the time, Zeke was driving back from Apalachicola with his wife and had plenty of time to talk.

"I'll only keep you a minute, but what I want to talk to you about is pretty important and I'm going to need your help."

I arrived back at the store in time to see the taillights of Matt's car driving away. *Rats.* I hated missing him. I put the hamburger meat into the fridge and sat down to ponder the events of the past few days. I'd seen very little of Jessica since our trip out to Tate's Hell. I was also chomping at the bit to tell her about Delia and her strange behavior.

When Jessica pulled in with Grandma, I stood and watched as they walked up the steps.

"You're doing great, Grandma," I said, observing how well she did. "Look at you, the way you took those steps."

"Yes, and after that long ride. I've never seen the likes of it," Jessica bragged, "someone recovering from sepsis like this. It's practically a miracle."

Grandma Rosella waved the comments aside. "I've got all my children around me. That's what it is. Having you around is a healing balm." Grandma had a way of calling us all children.

I gave her a big hug, careful not to knock her off balance, and we all walked into the kitchen where my steaming shepherd's pie was out of the oven and ready to serve.

"Mmm, that smells good," Jessica said. "But Millie's fixed food too, and I need to get over there."

"I'll miss you, sis," I said. "We've got so much to talk about."

"Sure do. I'll call you in a few."

A couple of minutes later she did call—from a parking lot, she said. I stepped away from the kitchen as she filled me in.

"It's not that Mama wouldn't tell me who my father is," she said. "Mama doesn't even know."

"Oh, Jessica..."

"Listen, I'm just going to let it drop. No DNA, no chasing things down. It's me and Mama, and that's that. It's just the way things are for me."

"Wow, Jess. How unexpected. I wish I had something to say that would help."

"There's you guys, too. I've got you all," Jessica said. "So it's okay. It's got to be okay. There's nothing I can do about it. And tell Grandma Rosella she was a big help, with some of the things she said before we got there. Please thank her for me. I don't think I was good company on the way back, trying to process it all. And I didn't thank her.

"I'll sure tell her," I said. "She'll be happy to hear it."

34

The colorful morning faded to the glaring white of noon, and Sol continued his trudge toward Carrabelle. He regulated his pace to conserve energy and coddle the blisters between his toes. Whenever a car passed, which were very few, he stuck out his thumb. But nobody picked him up. He sighed and figured he could walk all the way to Carrabelle if he had to. He didn't care. He'd make it with or without help. He just hoped he made it before his mom died.

Water-filled swales lined both sides of the road like mirrors and reflected a blue sky. Every now and again, Sol descended the embankment to sit and rest. He dipped his hands into the puddles and drank as much as he could of the sun-warmed water. If it gave him diarrhea again, or parasites, Sol would just have to deal with it. At least the ditches weren't swimming with gators.

But as time passed, he grew wearier, and those stops became more and more frequent. During one of these stops, Sol lay down in the water, fully clothed, and floated there, rinsing off the sweat. He wasn't too proud, no sir, not after all he'd been through the last few days.

In the meantime, Sol still kept his eyes peeled for any sign of blueberries. He ate some of what he found and, careful not to overeat, he stuffed his pockets with the extras. After all, people could survive for days without food.

He lifted his shirt and examined the welts and scratches covering his pale belly, mostly from last night's stay in the tree. His pants, loose now, didn't want to stay up. Dropping his shirt tail he decided not to torture himself by thinking of hunger or his increasing weakness or the lightheaded spells he was beginning to feel. At least he was back on the road. This was big progress, even if he was slowing down.

When he rose, he took off his flip flops and walked for a while along the soft grass, tall now from all the rain. Blisters burned between his toes. Going barefoot wouldn't take him very far, but it gave his feet a break. At least the gator hadn't eaten his flip flops last night.

He raised a hand and fingered the bandage around his head. It had to be filthy. He wondered whether it hurt his chances for hitching a ride, but he left it alone to keep the bugs away from his stitches.

A vehicle approached from behind. Sol turned briefly to catch a glimpse and then stuck out his thumb. And just like the other night, a truck pulled over on the shoulder.

Sol swallowed, remembering the first one and wondered whether he should just pass on by and forget about trucks in general.

He took a chance and stopped at the passenger door. Because of the slope of the shoulder, he could barely reach the door handle.

The bearded young driver leaned toward him. "Come on around," he said, "hop in the back."

Sol came around to the driver's side but before he could climb in the guy rolled down his window and stuck his head out, "Where you goin'?"

"I'm heading to Carrabelle."

"Carrabelle?" His voice sounded incredulous. "Carrabelle is behind you, buddy. In that direction." He pointed back to where Sol had come from.

Sol gripped the side of the truck and closed his eyes. The whole world seemed to spin.

"Say, buddy, you ain't lookin' so good. Let me pull around to where I can pick you up better. And I'll drive you back thataway."

Sol took his hand off the truck while the guy made a three-point-turn on the level asphalt. He opened the passenger door from inside and gave it a shove.

"Thanks," Sol croaked. It was all he could do to climb up into the seat. He leaned back and heaved a sigh. "Finally," he said. "I finally made it outta there."

The driver, in his muscle-tee shirt and huge tattooed arms, shifted gears and took off down the road. "You ain't lookin' too good, man. What's goin' on with the bandage and all?"

"Oh, that was a while ago. But since then, I've been lost in the woods. For days."

The guy pointed toward the palmettos with an expression that seemed to say, "In there?"

Sol nodded. "Got any food? Anything at all?"

The guy swung an arm around to the backseat and came back with a sandwich and bottle of cold water. He held them out to Sol.

Sol took them. "Thank you, man. Thank you." His hands trembled as he fumbled open the cellophane and bit off a quarter of the sandwich. "Thank you again," Sol said.

"You must be starvin'. Don't make yourself sick, now," the man said as Sol practically poured the cool water down his throat.

"Ahhh, you don't know how good this is," Sol said, admiring the now empty bottle.

"You want another?" The man didn't wait for a response but brought up another sandwich and drink.

"I don't wanna eat your lunch," Sol said.

"Forget it. Glad to help."

A twinge of nausea did force Sol to slow down. About halfway through the next sandwich, he spotted something up ahead—a dark-colored car parked along the side of the road. "Hey," he said wiping his mouth on the back of his hand and pointing as they passed. "That's…" he paused to get a closer look at the paint and license plate, "that is my car. Can you pull over?"

The young man braked and then backed up until he was even with the car.

Sol climbed out. He reached back in and shook the man's hand. "Thank you, friend. I'll be fine now. I'm very much indebted."

"You sure I can't do something else for you?"

"All good now. Thank you very much."

"Anytime," the man said with some hesitation. "You take care now." Then he pulled forward and made a three-point-turn to go back from where he came.

Sol waved as the truck headed into the distance. But he couldn't help feeling a sense of unease. He shook it off. At least he was back at his car. That's all that counted, right?

As the truck's taillights disappeared around a curve, he lifted the other half of his sandwich toward the sky. "And thank You, God."

Only then did it occur to Sol that his car door might be locked. "Nooo!" He bolted for the door handle and gave it a yank. It swung open, and Sol breathed a sigh of relief.

He stood outside the door and tightened the lid on his half-empty bottle of water and then tossed it in with the sandwich onto the passenger seat. But they didn't smack Eddie's plastic blue upholstery, they fluffed against soft shreds of foam stuffing and ribbons of blue plastic—the trashed remains of former seat covers. Sol leaned in and stared. Debris lay everywhere, seats, floorboards, the dash. It was clear that an angry knife had inflicted the damage. Term's Atlas, his special keepsake, lay bent and torn up in the far corner of the passenger floor.

"Doggone it!"

Considering the damage, he'd better walk around and check the paint. With great trepidation, he eased around the car, eyeing every square inch. Not a scratch anywhere. Back at the driver's side, he shook his head. A miracle.

Then a thought hit. "The keys!" As he dove in behind the wheel, the dangling keyring slapped against his knee. "Yes!" He pumped his fist. At least the guy hadn't thrown them into the woods.

Then Sol remembered his money under the floormat. He stuck one foot out onto the grass and pulled it up. "Yes!" More good news. At least he could eat.

And the trunk. He popped the switch and jumped out. If his suitcase wasn't back there, he'd....

But it was.

He shut his eyes in gratitude, lowered the lid, and then climbed back in and turned the key.

The engine turned over, but wouldn't start.

He tried again.

And then he laughed.

No wonder the guy was mad. He'd run out of gas too.

By now, Sol was exhausted. With the window half down, he picked up the other half of his sandwich, leaned back and began to nibble. He unscrewed the lid on his water and took a sip and then took a few more bites. He reached into his pants pocket and pulled out a few half-smashed blueberries and gave them a chew. He listened to the birds outside and tipped the seat back. He'd just lie here a while and figure out what to do. But right now, he was too tired to get out on the road and thumb a ride. Just too tired…

The woods were dark when Sol finally cracked his eyelids open. A half-moon peeked back at him through the front window. He shut his eyes again and decided to let things go. He'd deal with it all tomorrow.

35

Sol awoke to a loud pounding on the window next to his head, and the sun in his eyes. He squinted and blinked trying to place where he was. He was in a car. Then he remembered, this was his— no—Eddie's vehicle. His shirt was drenched with sweat. And the seats… He glanced down at the ripped upholstery. The banging continued.

He shielded his eyes and turned left toward the racket, and there stood a massive silhouette with his hands on his hips. Morning sun blazed out from under the man's armpit. Sol raised the back of his reclined seat and leaned in to see, but still couldn't see the man's head. He was big, though. Mighty big.

"Sol? Time to wake up. Come on out of there."

Term? Couldn't be. But it sure sounded like him.

Sol opened his door and stepped out, still squinting and shielding his eyes. "Term?" He threw himself against the giant and gave him a hug and then stepped back again. The man still reminded Sol of the character in that *Terminator* movie. "Man, I've missed you. You can't believe how glad I am to see you. Where've you been?"

Term grinned down at Sol like the Jolly Green Giant but said nothing.

"When you left, I thought I'd never… So, how'd you get here?"

Term gave him a wink. "Guess I just flew in," he said. Then he stepped back and pointed to his red Jeep parked up ahead on the road's sloping shoulder.

"Oh, man, you would not believe…" Sol began.

"Yes, I would. You look terrible."

Sol reached up to his nearly forgotten bandage. When he brought his hand back down a lump of yellow foam clung to his fingers. He flicked it off.

Term then strode toward the Jeep on his long legs. "Come on over here. I've got something that might be yours."

The man was three or four paces away when Sol took off after him. "What I'm hoping is that you've got some gas."

"Did you pray for some?" Term asked over his shoulder.

Sol caught up to him. "Uh, I haven't…"

Term opened the back of his vehicle and pulled out a gas can. He set it on the ground and turned back and reached inside a box on the floorboard. He pulled out a bottle of water, bag of steaming hot breakfast sandwiches, a wallet, and a cell phone. "The phone's got a dead battery, but would you like these back? And some breakfast?"

Sol's mouth dropped open. "How'd you…"

Term grinned and handed him his belongings. He watched as Sol stuffed his phone and wallet into his pockets and then gave him the food and water. "You doing okay?"

Sol opened his mouth, but nothing came out. Term lifted the gas can and motioned with his head for Sol to follow. He emptied its contents into Sol's gas tank while Sol dropped his bag of breakfast onto his front seat. When Term finished pouring, he extended the can toward Sol.

Sol reached out, but Term held tight, his face reflecting an expectation for Sol to say something.

"Thank you, Term. Very much. And I know, I know," Sol said. "I'll be sure to pass it on."

"Okay then." Term let go of the can.

Sol fitted the empty red container into his trunk next to his suitcase and shut the lid. "I sure appreciate this, man, I don't know how you…"

"You're welcome. Now, are you ready to follow me into Carrabelle?" He pointed to Sol's front door. "Hop in. When we get there, watch, and I'll give you a signal where you can find your son."

Sol scrambled in on top of the shredded seat. He turned the

key, and the engine fired right up. Aside from the sound of Term's voice, the noise of the engine was the best sound he'd heard in a long, long time.

It didn't take Sol long to wolf down the breakfast sandwiches and water. He followed the red Jeep into Carrabelle and realized the distance wasn't very far after all. The vehicles took a right fork, then a second right fork onto Highway 98 and before long appeared a little green sign that said *Carrabelle.*

Term kept the pace slow and steady, and when Sol glanced down at his speedometer to see what speed they were going, he noticed his gas gauge.

Full?

But Term only had a…

Up ahead of Term's, brake lights flared.

Sol tapped his brakes.

Term stuck his arm out the window and pointed over to the right.

Sol turned to see what it was.

And there stood his wonderful son Matt beside a cut-up log splitting wood like a lumberjack with some fancy device. Matt's face and muscular arms were tanned now, like he'd been out in the sun. A lot.

But when Sol turned toward Term's Jeep again he gasped. The taillights he'd followed into Carrabelle had continued up and over the bridge.

Sol's heart sank. "Term! No. Don't leave, man!" he yelled.

Nonetheless, he twisted the steering wheel toward his son and his stack of firewood.

And boy, oh boy, was he glad to see Matt.

Sol parked the car and climbed out. "Matt!" he hollered.

Matt turned away from his work and stared at his dad. "Dad?" He didn't seem to recognize him.

"It's me, Matt, your dad."

Matt dropped his work and raced toward Sol. He hugged him, lifted him off the ground, and then set him back down. "Where have you been?"

Sol's eyebrows rose, and he blew out a breath.

Matt leaned back and studied the bandage around Sol's head. "Dad, what happened to you?"

Sol shrugged. "Too much to go into right now." He pulled at the bandage, but it wouldn't let go. "Help me pull it off, Matt. It's stuck."

Matt turned him around backward and tugged the matted blood loose from his hair. "Dad, this thing is nasty. And stitches?"

"Tell you later," Sol said and took the bandage away, wadding it in his hand. "Guess I don't need it anymore."

Matt hugged him again. "It's good to see you. Peter and I were ready to send out a search party."

Sol shook his head. "I'll explain it all, but you're not going to believe it when I tell you."

Matt gave him a long look. "I want to hear every word of it. Have you eaten? You look—you look awful."

Sol waved it off. "Yeah, I ate."

"Then how about a shower?"

"I need to see your grandmother, Matt. First thing. That's the whole reason I came."

"Dad. No. First, you can't go see her looking like this. You'll scare her to death. And…listen to me now. You're not going down there to harass her. I won't let you."

Sol hung his head. "I wasn't planning to. I just want to see that she's okay."

"She's okay. She's real okay."

Sol nodded. "Good then."

"She'll be here after you get cleaned up. Now let's go get your stuff. You can get cleaned up in my cabin. Are you sure you don't need something to eat? I've never seen you like this. You're beat-up. Skinny. You've got stitches. And that scruff of a beard…" Matt stepped back. "You could trim that up, it might look pretty good."

Sol waved him off and stepped over to the car to open the trunk. Matt beat him to the suitcase and shut the trunk.

"You want me to walk you over in a bit?" Matt asked.

"It's just over there, isn't it?" Sol asked and pointed next door to the store.

Matt nodded.

Sol didn't need a babysitter. "You stay here and tend to your business."

Just then, another car drove up and parked beside Sol's vehicle. A slip of a girl with turquoise blue hair and a short skirt climbed out and sashayed toward them. Sol frowned. She passed by Sol without so much as a glance but paused to bat her eyes at Matt.

"How's my big boy," she purred and sauntered on by. At the door of a cabin, she stopped to glance back over her shoulder. She smiled at Matt who now had his back turned with a look of annoyance on his face.

Sol stared as the girl disappeared into the cabin. When the door shut, he turned back to Matt. "That's not—that's not your girlfriend, is it? The one you've been telling me about?" He hoped like the dickens it wasn't.

"No, Dad," Matt said, his lips clamped together. "That's nobody."

"Whew," Sol said, "had me worried for a minute."

36

The next morning, while Matt was out working on the tree, I learned his mom and dad had shown up. Because they all slept in, I hadn't had a chance to meet them.

So, I caught up with Jessica. "Come on down to the library with me."

In her current state of mind, Jessica was less than enthusiastic about visiting a library. But I knew she'd perk up when she saw the rack of cookbooks I had found.

As we walked in, I spotted the little old man I met the other day. Once again, he was on duty at his register. "Morning, Mr. Jessie," I said. "It seems you're the main attraction in here."

"Yes, these days it's mainly just me and old Coot, unless I get customers. In this room, anyway." He glanced down to the old yellow dog sprawled at his feet. I hadn't noticed the dog the other day. The lettering on his engraved brass dog tag said *Coot*.

"Hi, there, poochie," I said.

The old dog wagged his tail but made no effort to raise his head. I turned back to the elderly man. "And this is my good friend Jessica," I said. "Jessie meet Jessica. Jessica, meet Jessie." We all laughed.

"Nice to make your acquaintance," he said with a broad smile as we headed over to the bookshelves.

It didn't take long for Jessica to perk up when she saw all the cookbooks. She came out of her funk and loaded my arms with books, most of them a dollar or less. "Wow, this is a treasure trove," she said. "But I have to stop. This is all I can deal with." She slid half the books onto her own arms. "Let's go settle up with Mr. Jessie. I need to get back and help Millie again."

"When are you going to let me in on your secret project?" I teased.

"Don't worry. It won't be long. And I think you're going to like it."

"A hint? Just one? Please? Is it something to do with decorating?"

She cocked her head. "Maybe, yeah, you could say that."

"Millie's cabin? The restaurant?" I had to know.

She smiled and shook her head. "Sorry, Coral. Not going to tell you. Only one hint allowed. But I'll let you know as soon as we're finished, okay?"

I stuck out my bottom lip, pretending to pout, and she grinned.

"I'm glad you told me about these books." She heaved her load onto the counter, followed by mine. "I can't wait to try some new recipes up at Aunt Allie's. Maybe Mom will come down one day from Tallahassee and meet everyone. Now that she's met Rosella, I bet she will. We could make a special dinner."

Mr. Jessie rang up the books on his register.

"I'd love that," I said. "We could make it a party and invite everyone."

"That'll be twelve dollars and twenty-five cents," the man said.

Jessica opened her purse but came up short on cash.

I hadn't brought a purse.

"You'll take checks, right?" she asked.

"Oh, yes, we'll take whatever you have, cash, checks, credit cards."

She wrote out her check, and he began to fill out the receipt. "Sparrow," he said, commenting on her last name. "Same last name as mine. Not very common, you know."

"Do you have family here?" I asked as Jessica folded away the receipt. He slid the books into two brown bags with handles.

"Don't want to make it too heavy for you," he said and got back to my question. "The wife's gone. My only daughter left us years ago, ran off with a boy I didn't approve of, and made no further contact. So, it's just me and old Coot here, like I said." He seemed resigned to the situation. "And he's on his last legs, poor fellow."

"I'm sorry to hear about your family," Jessica said. "But I'm glad you've got your doggie. He's a sweet one." She bent over to stroke the canine's gray muzzle.

I took one of the bags from the counter. "What was your daughter's name?"

"Prissy. Sweet little Prissy."

That got Jessica's attention. "Prissy like in Priscilla?"

"The very same."

Jessica ignored the other bag on the counter and opened her wallet again with trembling fingers. She pulled up a picture of her mother on her phone and held it out. "Did she look anything like this?"

Mr. Sparrow drew the phone closer and squinted, bending close. His hands begin to shake. "Yes, she does. Dear Jesus." His voice quavered. "That's Prissy's crooked little smile. Who is this?"

"That's my mama. Priscilla Lee Sparrow," Jessica said, and putting it all together began to cry.

The old man's eyes welled up. "Oh, dear Heavenly Father. Is Prissy alive?"

Jessica nodded. "And I'm Jessica Lee Sparrow."

"And my name is Jessie Lee Sparrow." He opened his arms. "May I hug you?"

"My granddaddy? Are you kidding? Yes."

He looked down over her shoulder at the dog. "You hear that, Coot?" His voice cracked and a tear fell to the floor. "Prissy didn't hate me after all. She couldn't have." He sobbed, patting Jessica on the back and then leaned back and looked at her. "She named her baby after me." He stayed there looking into her face. "And she's a pretty little baby, too."

I knew then that it was God who emptied out the house the day before and left me lonely without a car. He's the one who led Grandma Allie to want to visit the library. And He had drawn me into that Friends of the Library room, and He let Mr. Jessie be on duty yesterday and today, and He made sure Jessica didn't have enough cash and had to write a check.

And now because of Him, Jessica had someone too.

Allie answered a knock at the side door. On the other side of the screen stood a man who introduced himself as Sol Flores. He said he'd arrived this morning to see his mother.

She studied him up and down and applied her less-than-hospitable stare. So, this was Rosella's son, the fellow with the nasty reputation. *Hmph.* Rather beat-up looking as far as she was concerned.

"I'm sorry, Mr. Flores. Rosella is taking a late morning nap." But she held open the door just the same. "You might as well come on in and wait. Have you eaten?"

He entered and thanked her. "You can call me Sol, ma'am. And, no ma'am, I haven't eaten. I wanted to see Mama first."

"Well, pull out a chair at the table. I'll fix you some fried eggs and toast."

After all, the fellow was Rosella's son.

Hmph. So far he seemed like any other person.

Regardless, Allie wasn't inclined to chit chat with a scoundrel like him, so she brought him a cup of coffee and left him to his thoughts as she stood over the stove and prepared his meal.

When she finished, she set the plate in front of him and sat with her own coffee on the opposite side of the table

He ate with enthusiasm.

"You act like you haven't eaten for three days," she said.

"Mmm, this is so delicious," he said. Several times he thanked her and then continued eating until he finished. He cleaned the last bit of yolk off his plate with a corner of toast and wiped his hands and mouth with a napkin. "And yes, ma'am, I might have skipped a few meals lately."

"You're welcome," she said, not entirely clear on what he was talking about. She rose to pour him another cup of coffee and wash his dish. The girls, gone now, had already cleaned the kitchen.

Coral and Rosella had forewarned Allie that his visit—something about Rosella's will—might bring trouble. Well, Rosella in her condition didn't deserve to hear all that, and Allie wasn't about to interrupt her nap. She'd wake up when she was good and ready, and he could wait it out.

As she lowered the warm frying pan into the water, sadness fell over her as she thought back to her dream about Rosella and the doves.

This morning nap was not the norm lately for her spunky Rosella and felt like a setback. She wondered just how little time she might have left with her friend and decided she wouldn't let this guy cut it short with his bad attitudes.

Allie dried her hands and stepped toward Rosella's bedroom door.

"Is that her room in there?" Sol wanted to know as she peeked in on her.

Allie nodded without turning. She noted the rise and fall of Rosella's breathing before easing the door shut.

Sol gestured toward the bedroom. "When I talked to Matt just now, he said she was doing really well."

"Rosella's tired today. And that worries me."

"You're mighty watchful, Ms. Bentley."

She sat down at the table again and took a sip of her cold coffee. "At times a dream comes true," she said. "And at times it doesn't, but it carries a hidden message." She wasn't going to mention the nightmare about the fire, either.

Sol didn't get it. He cocked his head as if to say, *What the heck?*

She left him to ponder her meaning.

"More coffee?" she said, mostly to get his mind off her comment. "You still hungry? Would you like some poor-man's pie?"

She filled his coffee again and dished him up a piece of last night's peach pie. He probably didn't cook, but she explained it anyway. "It's more of a one-of-each-pie," she said. "One egg, one stick of butter, a spoon of vanilla, a cup of sugar, a cup of flour, and a cup of fruit. Stir it up and put it in the oven at 350 until it's done." She laid out a fork as she placed his dessert in front of him.

"This looks fine," he said. And once again, he dug in with relish. *"Mm hmm."*

She assumed he'd only been half-listening, so his next question surprised her.

"So, you have dreams?"

"I do."

"Care to share?"

It wouldn't hurt anything to share an old one, like the one about her great-granddaughter. "Well, yes, I did have one come true. Sort of. I dreamed my granddaughter came back. I hadn't seen her in a long while—since she was little. And in the dream, she came right through the store's front door."

He shoveled in another bite and waited.

"The granddaughter didn't come back. But my *great*-granddaughter did. It wasn't exactly like the dream, though. The sun wasn't shining behind her back when she came through the door. *Hmm.* I hadn't thought about that before. But one night she actually did walk straight through that very same door. And it wasn't long ago."

Sol polished off his pie and nodded, zeroing in on her words now. He pushed the dish away and leaned on his elbows. "How long did it take? I mean, to come true."

Allie should have written the date. "A year—or two, perhaps. I don't know. But I believed it. Some dreams stand out. They feel important, and you just know. Like this one. And some dreams, you figure they're just entertainment."

He waved the story away. "Yeah, but it wasn't exactly your granddaughter, right? Life is full of coincidences."

So he was a doubter. "I had two more dreams. Just recently."

Sol perked up. "Yeah?"

She lifted his empty dish.

"For one, I dreamed the store burned down."

Allie motioned toward the coffeepot. "I need to go open my store and dust and sweep a bit. Make yourself comfortable and help yourself to more coffee and pie if you like."

As she turned around to head into the store, she caught Sol studying the naked bulb that hung over her table. He took in the wall switch with its antique black knob that required turning with the fingers.

As she stepped in to unlock the store, she considered how her words had affected him. She shouldn't have blurted out about the fire and hoped it didn't cause problems with his mother staying here.

She returned to the kitchen to find his coffee cup empty and him still sitting there with his feet crossed.

He continued the conversation as if she'd never left the room and seemed to be reassuring himself. "I'm sure the store will be all right, though, huh?" Then he chuckled a nervous sort of laugh. "So far, so good, right?"

Allie shrugged. She had no encouragement to offer. Her store was an old building.

"Maybe one day I can do something about all this," she said, "I'd certainly like to be able to afford new wiring. Some friends have made donations toward it. I haven't told Rosella. In the meantime, we're all being very careful."

Once again, she stepped over to the bedroom door and cracked it open to peek inside.

Sol came alongside and peered around her. "You just checked on her," he whispered. "Is there something going on that I should be worried about?"

Allie closed the door. "She's getting better by the day. But she's my friend. Friends look in on their friends."

"But—well, I'm glad you're here for her," he sputtered. She sensed it embarrassed him that she had taken the lead in being concerned.

"She did say she was tired," Allie told him. "And these last few days have been a bit crazy."

"It's all the fuss—about me coming in and all," Sol said. "It's worn her out, I guess."

Allie hoped that was all.

"So…" he began. "You said you had another dream?"

For a doubter he is quite persistent. Allie gazed into his face. There was no way she was going to tell him about that other dream, the one with the doves flying out of Rosella's fingertips.

She truly hoped the dream had some other meaning besides death.

37

Sol rose as his mother appeared at the bedroom doorway. After that eternal wait with Ms. Bentley, it was nearly noon. Sol finally insisted the woman wake his mother up. Either she would, or he would.

"I've got to talk to her," he said. "I've come a long way—a very long way—and it's important."

So Allie conceded. "I will do it," she said, "Just so you know, I don't like it, but she *is* your mother. I still think she needs her rest."

"She'll get caught up. And I think what I say is going to help," Sol said.

Allie didn't respond, but by the look on her face, he got the feeling she didn't believe a word of it.

At the doorway of her room, his mother paused and smiled as her eyes landed on his. He grinned and stepped forward to give her a big hug. Then he guided her by the elbow over to the dining table. She fussed about it, but Sol insisted.

Meanwhile, Allie disappeared onto the porch.

Sol seated his mama next to the table with her chair facing his.

"Sol," she said as she sat down. "It's so good to see you, Son." Then she got a closer look at his face. Concern clouded her eyes. "What's happened to you, Sol?

"I-I'm…" By now he'd taken a good look at her, too. "Mama. You've lost w…" He stopped himself. "But you're looking good, Mama. Real good." He leaned forward and gave her a kiss on the forehead.

Her expression turned sad. "You thought I'd die, didn't you?"

That hurt, but Sol knew he deserved it. He cleared his throat. "I-I wanted to talk about that."

Ms. Bentley wasn't far away, and he knew she could hear every-thing they said through the screen door.

"It's all set, I'm not changing executorship, Sol."

"No, Mama, not that. I don't care about that."

Rosella frowned and studied his face. She seemed to be trying to get a handle on where he was coming from.

"Do whatever you want with that," he said. "Matt and the neigh-bor girl, they can settle things any…"

She stopped him. "You don't need to call her the neighbor girl anymore. She's Matt's girlfriend."

"Fine. I understand. Let them do whatever they want to do." He lifted her hands in both of his. "Mama. I'm sorry. I'm so sorry."

She remained silent.

"Mama, I haven't been good to you. I know it now. And I want to set it straight."

She seemed to understand now what he was talking about. "Son, I always forgave you."

He brought her hands closer to him. "I-I had to tell you that. In person. Before you… I was so hateful. All the time."

"And I still forgive you, honey."

"You…you've always treated me like…well, an angel."

Rosella laughed at that. "Not so fast. I'm just a person who loves her son and am always praying for him."

"I love you, too, Mama. And I know after what I've been through, somebody had to be praying."

He kissed her hands, tears in his eyes and sobbed. "I was afraid I wouldn't get to tell you." Tears rolled down his face. "I'm so sorry."

After the visit with his mother, Sol returned to Matt's cabin where his son was still sweating and splitting firewood. "You look like a regular pioneer out here," Sol said. "I should be helping you."

"C'mon, Dad. You're in no shape to do this."

Sol shrugged. He knew he wasn't up to it. "Not today, anyway. Were you able to get my phone charged up?"

Matt swiped at his nose to get the woodchips off his face. "By the way, I called and got you a room at the B & B next door."

"Good thinking, son. I appreciate it."

"You'll be upstairs in room three. And we're all meeting at the restaurant tonight. So put on your best clothes. It's an engagement party for Ralph and Millie, people you're going to like."

Sol lifted his arms and showed Matt his outfit, a clean Hawaiian shirt and Bermuda shorts. "This is my best. Good enough?"

"Guess so," Matt said. "Your phone is plugged in beside the door. Want me to walk you over to the B & B?"

"Nah, no need to babysit me, Matt. I'll get my suitcase."

"I found your clothes and put them in a plastic bag. If you want, I'll put them in the washer with mine."

"I've got a few more," Sol said as he stood by the door.

"And those blueberries in your pockets? What was that about?"

Sol laughed and ducked inside. He came out with his phone and suitcase. "That's part of the story," he said, shutting the door. "It's a doozy, son. And you're gonna think I'm lyin' through my teeth when I tell you."

Sol stepped around his vehicle with his suitcase and crossed the street to the B & B next door. But as he approached its steps, a tall attractive redhead backed out and was securing the lock. She almost looked like… And then she turned.

"Paulette?"

She turned and stared before recognition set in. "Sol? It's you!" She came forward and gave him a big hug and then stepped back to look him over. She shook her head. "What in the world happened to you?"

Just then a young man backed out the door and secured the lock again. Busy place. But when the young man turned, Sol realized it was Eddie.

"Eddie? Great day. Did everybody in Las Vegas come down? Wow. This is a surprise. What brings you all here of all places?" Sol wanted to know.

"Eddie," Paulette said, "was hoping to drive his car back."

"I wasn't stealing it, Paulette."

"No, it was part of the deal I made to get him to fly down. I forced him take a few days off," Paulette said. "Paid, of course."

Sol wasn't about to fly. "I'm not going back in a plane."

She shook her head. "No need. We're all driving back together."

Hmm, that sounded cozy. "I guess that's what happens when someone else is runnin' the store, huh? Thank you, Paulette."

She stared at him with a look of disbelief. "You're welcome."

In the past, Sol would have complained or accused her of trying to take over.

He set the suitcase down on the ground. "But why are *you* here, Paulette?"

"Like I said, I'd only come back if you changed."

He gave her a look that said *okaaay* and turned to Eddie. For now, he had no idea what Paulette was talking about. "Say, Eddie…" He pulled out his keys and dangled them. "Wanna try out your car?"

"Yeah, sure!" The kid reached for the keys and glanced around at the parking lot. "But where'd you park it?"

Sol laughed and pointed across the street at the parking space in the front of the first cabin.

Eddie's mouth flew open. "Is that it?" He stared back and forth between Sol and the shiny maroon vehicle with the glittery black racing stripe and new tires. "No way!"

"Yes, way."

Eddie started to bolt across the street, but Sol grabbed his arm. "Look, whatever you see inside, it's a long story. But I'll fix that for you too. Don't be shocked. Just—just giving you a heads-up, okay?"

"Right!" Eddie said and took off across the asphalt. "This is fantastic, Sol. Thanks!"

"You made that kid's day," Paulette said.

And Sol grinned. He felt pretty good, too.

Sol picked up his suitcase. "Let's go sit on the porch here," he said as Eddie backed up and headed east on the highway.

She followed him up the steps again, and they sat together on the wicker love seat. "First," Paulette said, "has Matt told you there's a get together tonight down at the restaurant?"

"He mentioned it."

"Wear some nice clothes," she said. "It's a party."

"On the way back to Las Vegas," Sol said, crossing his foot over his knee. His legs were all scraped up, so he uncrossed them again. "There's people I want you to meet. But shoot…" He turned and looked back across the bridge where Term's red Jeep had disappeared. "I'm sorry you didn't get to meet my friend Term."

"Friend?"

He gave her a look. "I can have friends. I have a lot of friends, Paulette." He thought back to when he confessed to Term that he didn't have any. Well, that was before. "I do."

She nodded, a smile on her face.

"On the way to Florida there was this kid—a cute little Mexican boy, maybe four—he followed me around like a puppy. Played pranks on me." Sol turned to Paulette. "Poor little thing. He broke his leg, and there I was carryin' him down the street and him cryin' and hangin' onto my neck all the way down to the clinic. Couldn't even speak English."

"Mexican, huh?" Paulette continued smiling.

Sol crossed his arms and gazed down at the broken sidewalk. "We'll have to stop by and see him on the way home. You'll—you'll really like him—his family too."

"I'm sure I will."

"I just wish you could've met Term. He was there."

He turned back to Paulette, who seemed to be enjoying his story. "And then there's the young mother and her son—spittin' image of Matt when he was little—hey, have you seen Matt yet?" Then he thought better of it. "I guess you have. He told you about the party."

She nodded. "I did, but I haven't bothered him. He's working right now. Finish your story."

Sol took her hand and looked into her beautiful green eyes. "Paulette, all I've done is think about you this whole trip and what you said about not coming back home until I'd changed."

Her smile widened, and her eyes crinkled at the corners.

"So please tell me what I need to do. I want you back, honey. I want us to be a husband and wife like we shoulda been the whole time."

She laughed and kissed him on the cheek. "You are so oblivious!"

"Okay," he said, "so just tell me what I need to change."

38

Millie set the soda down in front of Matt. He leaned against the wall at the end of the booth with his leg propped along the seat. He looked exhausted.

"Poor kid. You tired?" she asked.

"Worn out."

She felt bad that he'd slaved all day on that tree in her yard. But he should be done before long. Ever since Ralph rented him that longer chainsaw and log splitter, she'd noticed faster progress. His father had even stepped over to help him stack wood today. Aunt Allie was going to be happy with all her mountain of firewood.

"How much longer on the tree?" Millie asked.

Matt shook his head. "Soon," he said. "But right now I can't even think about it. Got any apple pie?"

"You bet, honey. Comin' right up." She started toward the kitchen but turned back. "Now Matt, don't you let a piece of pie ruin your appetite, we've got that big meal comin' up."

He grinned. "No worries."

Every person near and dear to Millie and Ralph was invited to the engagement celebration tonight: the grandmas, Jessica and her grandpa along with Coot, his dog. Then there was Coral, Matt, Matt's dad and mom, and a few more. And right now, Jessica, who came early, was puttering around in the back dining room setting the tables with flowers and fancy silverware.

Millie returned with Matt's pie, a fork, and a napkin. "Where's your mom and dad? And Coral?"

"They're coming." Matt had already cleaned up. Millie thought him extra handsome in his button-down shirt and khakis.

175

Just then Delia popped in the front door wearing nothing more than her usual scant shorts and a low-cut tank top. Millie noticed and leaned close to Matt. "Look out, Matt," she whispered, "blue alert."

The girl cast her eyes around the restaurant and spotted Matt. She pranced on in and aimed straight for his table where she plopped down across from him. "*Mmm, mmm, mmm,*" she said. "Aren't you medicine for sore eyes?"

"I gave you tonight off, Delia." Millie interrupted her foolishness.

"A girl's gotta eat supper, though." She gave Matt a knowing wink. "Isn't that right, good-lookin'?"

Millie took out her pad. "So what'll you have?" She wished her gruff words would work on this bimbo.

Delia waved her arm in a circle and then lowered a finger at Matt, "I'll have whatever he's having." As if Matt would buy her a meal.

Not if Millie had anything to do with it.

She gave Delia a hard stare for about ten seconds. But even that didn't phase the shameless girl. Matt slid his soda and pie to the outer end of the booth and started to climb out. But Millie had another thought. Ralph had had a belly full of this girl too, and he was right back there in the kitchen. Millie blocked Matt's knee and pushed his foot back with a wink. "Stay there, honey. Your dish is coming right up."

Of course, Matt had no dish coming up, but he would catch on.

Ralph would have a solution.

He'd better, anyway. And real quick before Coral came down here and saw this girl at Matt's table.

Millie pivoted and returned through the swinging kitchen doors in search of Ralph.

Matt looked down at his pie and picked up the fork. All the while, Delia's presence radiated out from across the table like some radio-active thing he wanted to flee. If it hadn't been for Millie, he'd be sitting in the breakroom with this little snack. He should have done that to start with.

"I just love to see a big strong man cut wood like you do," Delia said. "It's…so macho."

"I told you," Matt said, swallowing, but not looking at her. "I have a girlfriend. There are plenty of other guys around."

"Not that I want any of them."

Matt took a deep breath and another large bite of pie. Best to gulp it down fast and get out of here. "Anyway, that's not how you should act to get a boyfriend."

She gave him a frown, crossed her arms, and leaned back for the first time. "Listen. I know the score. From way back. My dad, my grandad—and you, you're all on the same page. Only one thing makes you tick."

Matt wanted to roll his eyes, but he restrained himself. He didn't want to be rude.

Delia leaned forward and grinned. "I know you're busy with a girlfriend and all, but—I just love those sweet old dimples of yours."

Matt finished off the last bite of pie and kept his thoughts to himself. The girl just did not get it.

Millie burst through the restaurant's kitchen door. "Ralph, Ralph," she whispered, and hurried over to his side.

He turned around from the fryer.

"You're not going to believe this," she said and tugged him over to the pick-up window. She pointed toward the booth where Delia sat across from Matt. The poor guy was making a brave effort to finish off his pie while trying to ignore Delia. Millie explained what just happened.

"Little witch," she said. "How can we run her off?"

"*Hmm.*" Ralph frowned and considered the situation. "So, she wants what Matt's having?" He stepped around the stainless-steel table and glanced down at the four-foot shark laying there. A fisherman friend of Zeke's had just caught it and dropped it off. Larry was just getting set to process it.

A look of mischief passed over Ralph's face as he grabbed the meat cleaver, and *Bam! Bam! Bam!* chopped off the creature's head.

Millie nearly jumped out of her skin.

He set the cleaver on the table and turned to Millie.

"I've got just the thing," he said. "Go back in there…" he lifted his hands, "and act real sweet. Tell her we're out of Matt's dish. But then say you'll bring her out something just as good, a brand-new dish we're trying out and would like to get her feedback on it."

Millie gazed from the shark's head to Ralph. She smiled. Ralph raised his brows and gave her a conspiratorial grin. "Larry!" he yelled over his shoulder. "Come 'ere a minute. And hurry it up."

He turned back to Millie. "Make sure and keep Matt there. But call Coral and tell her to take her time. The party's going to be delayed about fifteen minutes.

Millie returned to the dining room to find Matt done with his pie and looking miserable. Delia seemed overly happy. She probably thought she and Matt would be getting acquainted soon. It was all Millie could do to act nice to the girl, but she followed Ralph's instructions. She apologized to Matt for the delay on his dish, but slipped him another wink and a hand gesture that told him to hang on a minute.

Matt responded with a nod. He understood.

Ralph huddled with Larry over at the fryer. Then Larry straightened and gave his boss a high five and a big smile.

Millie kept busy in the dining room as she waited for Ralph's signal that the shark's head was fried and ready. Within a few minutes, Ralph double-tapped the bell for Millie to come pick up Delia's special meal. On the platter sat a crusty brown shark's head with big black eyes that stared at the ceiling. One of the boys had popped in a pair of black olives. Rows of razor-sharp teeth lined its gaping mouth. Kale and baby tomatoes embellished its perimeter. Millie snickered. "Tell Larry it's perfect."

Millie gave a shiver as she picked up the dish. It was almost too ugly to carry. And as she approached the table, she had to hold her breath to keep from laughing. She slid the monstrosity onto the table with a flourish. "Your dish, Delia. I hope you enjoy it, compliments of the chef."

While Delia stared at the beast, Ralph came out of the kitchen and addressed Matt. "Matt, your girlfriend is here, along with her two Grandmas. They'll need some help getting out of Jessica's car."

"Sure." Matt took the hint and made his break from the table. He followed Ralph down the hall to the side door, leaving Delia alone.

Millie glanced back at the girl as she headed back into the kitchen.

Delia, now on her feet, stared down at the shark's toothy grimace. She backed away and made a beeline for the exit.

Millie doubted the girl would be back tonight.

39

The next morning, after Dad and Millie's engagement dinner, I stepped out of the house intent on chatting with Millie down at the restaurant.

Along the way, I stopped by to see Matt while he worked on the log. Piles of sawdust littered the ground. Thanks to better equipment, more of the tree's sections were disappearing by the day. And now, with Eddie's help, the employee that Matt's mom brought along, Grandma's stack of winter firewood was piling high on the far side of Cabin Three. I'd even heard my dad mention building a little lean-to to protect it from rain.

Matt stepped over to greet me. "Morning, Coral. How's my love?"

I smiled and leaned in for a kiss. We chatted a minute about the work, and I asked if his dad was all right this morning considering all those crazy stories he told us last night. The man had been through a lot.

"He should come out soon," Matt said. "I'm pretty sure he slept in."

"Poor thing."

"Yep, completely worn out."

Matt gave me another kiss, and I waved a good-bye to Eddie before I headed over the bridge toward the restaurant. But all the while, my heart struggled with the thought—the concern, rather—that Delia, Matt's persistent predator, might show up once again while he was working.

Matt only had eyes for me, I was sure, and I knew he was completely annoyed with her—but I guess what disturbed me was her shameless gall.

And I didn't like the way she'd hijacked space in my head.

Down at the restaurant I opened the door and slipped inside. The greatest part of the breakfast crowd had left by now, and in the quiet, I took a seat at my favorite booth.

My immediate thoughts were on pancakes and honey, but more than that I wanted—no, needed—a few minutes with Millie. After all, she was going to be a part of my life—my stepmother. I adored Millie but would still have to get used to the idea of having a stepmother. If I were to choose one for myself, though, I could think of no one better.

Last night at the party, Millie and I sat a little too far apart to chit chat. It seemed like everyone was talking at once, and there were so many there with exciting news to talk about, Millie and my dad, of course, then Jessica's grandfather—and Paulette and Sol. Once Sol started in on what happened to him out in the woods, well, nobody wanted to change the subject. The party was fabulous and lasted for hours.

It frustrated me that Dad and Millie gave no plans about their wedding other than it would be sometime down the road. I wanted all the little details. Every woman carries an idea of what she wants in her ceremony. So this morning, I thought I would come down and at least find out about her colors, where and when the wedding would be, and how I could help.

But as I waited there in the booth, the sound of uproarious laughter filtered out of the kitchen. Millie's voice carried out of the kitchen along with those of the two boys, Larry and Jack. One of the guys said something like, "Tell it again."

Then Millie said something about peeking out her front door and some guy wiping the sweat off his chest with a wadded-up shirt. Considering the hilarity, something was mighty funny back there, and I had no idea who they were talking about. So I stepped over and propped my arms on the pick-up window ledge. I wanted to hear more.

Millie leaned a hip against one side of the aluminum table, while Larry and Jack stood on the opposite side. "Let me tell you," she said, "the girl had no idea I was there."

Millie slapped the table. "There she sat in those shorts up to here, with her fanny hanging out, arrangin' that checkerdy tablecloth just so over the log—"

The boys howled and slapped their thighs, but I was dazed. Millie had to be talking about Delia.

Millie wiped a tear with the back of her wrist and caught her breath. "Oh, and then came the sandwiches and drinks with the straws just right—"

Everything Millie said described the scene I'd spotted the other day. But I hadn't even noticed her standing there.

She continued, "And then, Matt—oh, you should have seen the look on his face when he turned around and saw her behind him. That shirt went back over his head so fast—"

That's when Larry glanced up and spotted me in the window. He pointed my way. "Tell her, Millie. You've got to tell her!"

Millie turned and gasped in a pleased way. "Coral, yes! Hold on, honey," she said and pushed her way through the double kitchen doors to grab my hand and tug me inside. "It's all right, honey. Come on back here with us. You'll love this." I stepped into the bright lights of the kitchen, half dumbfounded by what I'd already heard.

"All right now, you've got to hear this," she went on, as the boys nodded in agreement. "Your fella Matt is *the man,* I have to *say*! You would have been so proud of him." She gave my arm a squeeze as she said it and then leaned against the table again and dove back into her story. "Coral, we've—never mind—just listen to the rest of this."

The boys stood there grinning with their arms crossed.

Millie continued, dramatizing with her hands. "And dear Aunt Gussie, there she was with those legs crossed just like that and him totally not falling for it."

Millie crossed her arms to show his stance. "Stood there just like that."

She made her voice gruff like a man's. "'I can't be—whatever—I've got a girlfriend.'"

Larry slapped his knee. "Wish I coulda been there."

Millie kept going. "Your man turned right around and walked away."

"Whoooee," Larry said, "Tell her about the shark's head."

Jack threw a punch and turned in a circle.

Obviously, none of them could stand the girl.

"And do you know it still took her a while to get her picnic stuff together and get out of there? I've never seen the likes of it."

Then they told me about the shark's head.

Yes, I was glad to be reassured about Matt, my wonderful man, but the girl—I didn't know what to think. Not sure what overcame me, but a chord had been struck in my heart, and my tears just burst forth. I could not stop them, and with everybody frozen and gawking at me, I began to sob. I was so out of control, so embarrassed.

Millie wrapped her arm around me.

Then the restaurant's front door opened, and Larry, Jack, and Millie glanced up—new customers. "Uh, oh," Millie said, "back to work, everybody. I've got Coral. Larry, you get the people out front."

"I'm sorry, I can't help it," I blubbered.

She turned her attention to me again. "Honey, if you ever had any doubts about that man of yours, you can forget 'em. He's a good one, and rest assured, he was not one bit impressed with that little bimbo."

I shook my head and buried my face in my hands. Of course, I never should have worried about Matt. "It's not Matt," I sobbed.

"Well then, what is it?" Millie asked, completely drawn to the need and empathetic. "Come on back here to the breakroom with me."

I bawled all the way through the door.

I'm not a crybaby, not ever, but this thing about Delia hit me head-on like a truck.

Back in the breakroom Millie sat me down on the battered sofa with a handful of napkins from the container on the table. She shut the door and sat beside me waiting for me to compose myself.

"I-I-It's just the way everybody's making fun of her."

"Of Delia? She's awful, honey. She's been after your man."

I wiped my nose on the napkins. "I know that."

"Well—what is the matter?"

"It—" I gasped for air. "All I can think of is—is my mother."

"Your *mother*?"

I nodded. There was no way I could verbalize all my broken memories to Millie. Not in such a short time.

"All those men coming and going from our place."

"Men?"

"At night when she came home from work. I understand it now, but I was only twelve at the time. She was trash, a throw-away. To herself, to every man who came in that trailer. And so was I for that matter."

Millie stared at me. *"You?"*

"Not like Mama, no. Rosella stepped in. She kept me safe."

"Oh, that dear Rosella."

"I know," I said. "She—she loved my mom—and turned her around."

"I told Rosella about Delia," Millie said. "She's been praying for her." She sighed and mumbled, "I guess I should be too."

I looked up. "Rosella knows?" Some fine job I'd done of covering it up. "That girl's not a throw-away, Millie." More tears flowed. "No more than my mother."

Millie wrapped an arm around me and gave me a squeeze. "I'm so sorry, honey. I just wasn't thinking. I probably should apologize."

"My mother's life is written all over Delia."

Millie pressed her fist over her mouth and began to cry.

"But tell her," I said, "Tell her she matters."

Sol, exhausted from last night's engagement party for Millie and Ralph, dragged himself out of bed and threw on his same old clothes. Matt was right about him liking the couple. They were good people as well as all the other people there. And tonight, at sunset, was some other function they all had to attend—whatever it was. *Whew! Party, party, party.* He'd get the details from Paulette in a little while.

Where was she, anyway? Even though she'd dropped back into his life, so far, he'd seen very little of her.

Bleary-eyed, he slugged down a cup of black coffee at the B & B before heading out to visit his mother and Aunt Allie.

Along the way he passed by his son, once again dripping with sweat in his quest to dismantle the log. Eddie, just like yesterday, was retrieving the pieces and stacking them onto the pile.

"Morning, Matt," Sol said. "Once I get back from Mama's I'll come back and help you."

Matt let go of the giant wood-splitter, wiped the chips off his face with the bottom of his shirt, and then stepped close. "Dad, like I told you," he said in a quiet voice, "you're not looking so good. There's no way I'm going to let you over-exert. Why don't you just enjoy your vacation? Do something fun with Mom."

Sol brushed the scoldings aside. "Oh, I am. I am." He gave Matt a light cuff on the arm. "Don't stop working on account of me, Son. I'll see you in a little bit."

Right now, Sol had important business down at the store.

Sol could hardly wait to see his mom again. She'd enjoyed the party last night and so had Aunt Allie. But it had run late. He'd chauffeured the two of them back to the store in Jessica's car. It surprised him how good that little task made him feel. Seems like after dinner last night, Eddie wanted to walk Jessica home, so that worked out fine.

Sol stepped up to the store's front door and found it closed. No surprise. So he circled around to the side and knocked on the screen door. Ms. Bentley answered and invited him on in. She didn't seem as hesitant today.

"Thank you, ma'am, and how are you today?" he said. It occurred to him that he should try to use the polite terms his mama used to teach him. "Is Mama up?"

"Good morning, Sol, and I'm fine today, thank you. Have you eaten?" Sol couldn't remember people always wanting to feed somebody like this back in Las Vegas.

He shook his head. "Not yet, ma'am." He'd try to keep his polite words consistent. This was the south, after all.

"Well, then, have a seat in the chair here." He complied, thinking his mama might still be asleep.

Ms. Bentley stirred around in the kitchen, intent on fixing him something to eat. Over by the stove, she gathered a plate, a loaf of bread, and a carton of eggs. She pointed to the parlor next door. "Your mother's in there sewing if you'd like to step in. She's working on a quilt we're making together." She tossed him a glance and added, "You look tired today."

He stood again. "Thank you for the breakfast, ma'am, but let me go in there and say good morning to Mama first," he said. "Has she eaten?"

Sol considered the words that had just fallen from his mouth and puckered his brow. For him to ask after his mother's well-being, well, he couldn't remember ever doing that before. Not right off the bat. But the words felt right, and *has she eaten?* had fallen out without him even thinking. He gave his head a shake. What was happening to him?

His mama was delicate, though, and wasn't it a son's place to…? He'd have to give this oddity some thought.

Ms. Bentley chuckled. "We all ate, a long time ago."

He stepped into the other room and found his mother threading a needle.

"Hi, good morning, Sol," she said. "I'm glad you came over."

He gave her a kiss on the top of the head and asked about her quilt—and for the second time what she thought of last night. Then he told her he'd come back in a few minutes after he ate.

He reentered the kitchen where Ms. Bentley was buttering a piece of toast. "Now, where were we when I walked out, Oh, yeah," he said, remembering her comment on his being tired. "I guess I am a bit scroungy," he said. "But I'll be back to normal soon." She was well aware of his condition after last night's party.

She cracked three eggs into her sizzling oil and set a plate nearby. "So you enjoyed that party? You sure had some tales."

"It was a great time. I really enjoyed your friends Ralph and Millie."

"They're your friends now, too."

Sol nodded and gave that some thought. Friends. His list was growing. What had happened?

"Ms. Bentley," he said as she brought the plate over. "Can you sit down a minute? I'd like to talk about something."

"It's Aunt Allie," she said and pulled a chair out to sit across from him.

"All right, Aunt Allie it is. So, I have a question. How much have you saved up toward that rewiring job?"

She scowled and placed her hands on the table. "Now that's none of your business, young man."

Sol shook his head. "You don't understand."

"No, you don't understand," she said. "It's not polite to ask about another's finances."

"Well, I apologize. Let me start over. I'd like you to give your donors their money back."

Aunt Allie gasped and sat back in her chair.

He leaned forward. "You see, I'd like to pay for the whole thing— and get the ball rolling as soon as we can."

"Oh, my. The whole thing?" She gave him a good long look. "That is something. I don't know what to say. That's mighty big of you."

"But I'm going to need your electrician's name or his phone number."

<h1 style="text-align:center">40</h1>

I stepped out of Grandma Allie's back door and locked it up. Jessica had driven off earlier with Grandma Allie and Grandma Rosella. But after the stories Millie told me down at the restaurant—especially that one about the shark's head—I owed Matt a whole lot more trust than I'd extended.

At this point, I was feeling dumb for worrying about Delia. But I wasn't oblivious to the fact that there were Jezebels out there who didn't give up until they conquered their prey. Those poor guys.

But Matt, completely repulsed by her, had stood firm, not even tempted. On the contrary, he'd sent her packing and told her to get lost.

And the way Millie talked—she was mad at my dad for hiring Delia—she'd been after him this whole time. As well as Jack and Larry—who'd seen right through her as well. Bravo to them all.

In my defense, him talking to her at that picnic setup on the log certainly did appear shady. I guess you can't always trust your eyes.

I descended the wooden steps and passed through the old gate, latching it behind me. Matt had phoned me earlier in the day, but only for minute. "I'd really like us to take a walk to the beach this evening," he said. "There's something I'd like to talk about with you."

Talk with me about what?

I had no clue what he want to talk about—maybe an outing of some kind? Maybe something to do with my dad's upcoming wedding? Maybe he had info I didn't. Anyway, I'd never turn down a walk to the beach with Matt. I didn't get to see him enough as it was. And a walk did seem like a good way to clear my thoughts.

"How about you meet me at seven thirty over by Millie's tree?" he asked. "We can eat afterward."

Usually, he'd come over and get me. And it was a bit odd for him to set an exact time. And eating afterward? Very few places would be open at that hour. Maybe he planned to drive us down the coast. I wondered if Apalachicola had some late-night places to eat.

I bit my lip thinking about my earlier stupidity. Some things are better left unmentioned.

"And wear my favorite dress," he added.

Okay, then, he hadn't read my mind and couldn't be annoyed. But I still felt a bit wretched for letting myself worry about that hussy.

"Sounds great," I said

At seven twenty-nine, I headed around the building.

Matt stood near the root end of Millie's fallen tree and waited for Coral to appear. His heart warmed as she stepped around the corner of the store in her special yellow and white sundress—she even wore the yellow flower in her hair—the exact outfit she wore the first time he laid eyes on her—his bright angel.

She drew near and took his hand. "Why this outfit?" she asked. "It's a bit fancy for the beach, isn't it?"

He smiled down at her. "Because it's my favorite. Anyway, we have an event to attend after a while."

"Oh?"

He checked the time. An hour and a half until sunset.

"It's a surprise, and besides, I want to show you off." He lifted his left hand with the folded beach towel in it. "Don't worry. You won't get sandy. We have this."

Bing! A text. Matt slid his phone out of his pocket and checked the one-word message from Zeke:

ETA?

He paused at the apex of the bridge to answer. "Excuse me a second, Coral, it's Zeke. I have to respond."

Ten min

But it was no more than a guess.

Down at the beach, Zeke would keep an eye on Matt's things so nothing weird happened to them, and he'd duck out of sight by the time Matt and Coral arrived.

Matt held Coral's hand as they descended the bridge. To the left a cardboard sign on her dad's restaurant door said *closed for repairs*. Matt hoped Coral didn't ask for specifics. He mopped his brow. The afternoon felt warmer than usual, but Matt suspected it might have more to do with his nerves. At least there was a breeze to sweep the mosquitoes and bugs away. Thank goodness for that and for the shade across the road at this time of day. "Beautiful evening, isn't it, Coral, the way the shadows fall across the pavement." He glanced her way, hoping he didn't sound too corny.

But she nodded, "I always enjoy the walk along here, especially at this time of day." After that she was quiet, apparently wrapped in her thoughts.

Matt searched for something meaningful to say and came up empty.

Once again, he checked the time. He would have preferred to take the Mustang instead, but driving down to the beach would be too quick, and he needed the short delay for Zeke's sake.

Their ten-minute walk passed in record time. And now, a stone's throw ahead, appeared the beach parking lot with its little out-building and concrete picnic shelters. Each step felt dream-like as he passed by them and they entered the beach path together. He led Coral across the higher dunes to the right where he flipped open the towel in just the right spot. It floated neatly over the white sand. A soft breeze tossed her hair as she followed his gaze to the lowering sun behind them and the straight blue horizon. He studied her eyes, a reflection of the sky, as she looked into the distance.

"It'll be sunset soon," he said, "when the sun will color the sand all orange and gold." He scooped a handful to sift through his fingers, brushed them against his white pants, and grinned. "And—in a little while—we'll see all that from a new place. But when that happens, I want you to think back and remember us here. Together. In this very spot."

"I will," she said, smiling up at him with those ocean-blue eyes. "It's beautiful, and you're so poetic today."

"So I am. Would you like to sit down, m'lady?" he said, motioning her toward the towel. "And how could I not be poetic, my dear, when you are the one who colors my life like that very sunset?" His knees quivered as he settled close to her and leaned forward to give her a soft kiss.

Twin clumps of sea grass separated their towel from even higher sand between them and the parking lot. And so far, this evening, those dunes were vacant.

And just behind Coral's end of the towel lay the circle of shells. She hadn't noticed.

I wondered what Matt was up to—checking his watch those several times on the way down here and telling me to remember a sunset that hadn't quite happened—and calling me his sunset—to mark the close of something.

I couldn't make myself believe it had some hidden meaning, and it didn't match with his poetry. However, I knew he had good reason lately for us not spending as much time together as I would have liked. And then, my imagination could just be reading too much into a situation where he was simply trying way too hard to be romantic.

He wrapped his arms around his knees, and with a solemn face and sober voice began, "Coral…"

My heart twisted. That look on his face—it seemed too serious to be something good, and it threw me for a loop. No matter what he might say, though, I'd always love this man and be his friend. And if it came to it, I'd never forget him.

"I'm sorry," I blurted out. Might as well get it out there. I had been pretty dumb.

He gave me a cockeyed stare. "What are you talking about?"

His response told me a lot.

I shrugged, regretting I'd even spoken.

"No, no, sweetheart." He took my hand. "You've done nothing. It's me," he said.

I took a deep breath, trying to fathom what he was getting around to.

"I've spent so much time away from you on Millie's projects and then Ralph wanting me over in Tallahassee, and then Zeke… It's not you."

I reflected on the roller coaster of events from the last few days and tried to piece together what he was getting around to. But his next words brought me back.

"So, Coral, after our talk, I made you something—or rather had it made."

"Our talk?"

"Out on Aunt Allie's porch. When I asked you if your mother's gold coin gave you the creeps. Remember?" He reached into the pocket of his rolled-up pants, and out came a gold necklace and pendant—my gold coin, the one I discovered in the shell. He laid it across my hand.

"Oh, my goodness," I said, glancing up at him. "It's beautiful."

He smiled right back with those gorgeous dimples. "I'd say you're the one who's beautiful. Here. Let me put it on you."

I leaned forward as he attached it around my neck then planted a warm kiss on my lips.

And that sweet kiss let me know right then and there that I could forget all that other nonsense.

Matt attached the necklace around Coral's neck. But after the kiss he glanced past her and his blood ran cold. A girl with turquoise blue hair and a beach bag stood over by the rail fence along the parking lot.

Delia.

She caught Matt's frigid stare and remained where she stood.

"Oh, Matt, this is a wonderful gift." Coral said as he loosened his hold on her. "I had forgotten about the coin."

Matt gave the blue-haired intruder the stink-eye and turned back to Coral. "I thought of the setting when Ralph and I stopped at a jewelry store up in Tallahassee."

"I bet it was when he went to get Millie's ring."

"Certainly was." After that first glance, Matt made a strong effort to keep his gaze off Delia. He had no idea what she was up to and refused to let her presence interrupt his time with Coral. "Look— hold on." He jumped up and stepped away from the towel to retrieve a little kiddie shovel that Zeke had also left nearby.

From behind the fence Delia watched.

He avoided her stare to concentrate on Coral, yet it made his skin crawl to see her out of the corner of his eye. "There's something I want you to see," he told Coral. "But you'll have to dig for it."

"What?"

"Like treasure." He handed her the plastic shovel Zeke had conveniently left. "You can use this."

She laughed, "Wha…?" and wrinkled up her freckled nose.

"Don't worry. It won't be hard. And I'll help if you need me." He pointed out a seaweed X marked by Zeke. "X marks the spot," he said. "Start diggin', little lady."

"Matt, you are so crazy," Coral said. "But I love it." She paused and searched his eyes. "And I love you. So much."

He gave her a peck. "I love you, too, but that doesn't get you off the hook. Dig, little lady."

It took very little effort for the shovel to make contact with the red plastic lid of a container. She dug the sand off the lid and paused.

"What's in there?"

"Take the lid off." The plastic jug was the gallon-type found in restaurants with mayonnaise in them.

"Stuff Ralph and I found," Matt said, "at your granddad's campsite. Buried exactly like this. But at that time, it was in a big glass jar with a rusty lid."

Coral drew back, her face serious. "Oh, Matt, I don't want anything from that place. It's evil."

He brushed the sand off the red lid and popped it off. "Look down inside. See what's there."

Coral leaned forward and then backed away, her mouth agape. "Are you kidding?"

The container was more than half full of gold coins. "You know what that's worth? The value of gold continues to rise."

She shook her head. "Horace—and I'll never call that beast my grandfather—was an evil devil, and I don't want his money."

Matt took Coral's hand and wrapped it in his. "I know that," he whispered.

In the meantime, other silhouettes in Matt's peripheral vision began to line the fence between them and the parking lot. He forced himself not to look at them.

"I had a feeling you'd say that, but I'm a little ahead of you, Coral."

She started to speak, but he stopped her with a finger. "Hear me out on this. Knowing how you'd feel, Grandma Allie and I had a similar conversation about the coins. But she reminded me of the Bible verse, 'The wealth of the wicked is laid up for the just.'"

Coral gave him a dubious look.

"In the meantime, I had Grandma Allie and Grandma Rosella pray over this, to break the ties that bind—break all connections to it—and all curses—and now it's as if they are all brand new. Your dad and I even scrubbed them. Right out there in the fish-scaling station. Every single coin. And that fancy new jar, by the way, came from your dad's place. We destroyed the old one."

Coral made no move to retrieve the container.

"Thank you, Matt. I guess that makes me rich now."

"You don't look too happy about it."

She nodded. "But thank you. Thank you for...for..."

He leaned forward and gave her a hug . "Here, here. I thought it might freak you out a little. But it'll be all right."

With his arm still around her, he glanced at his watch. Out in the parking lot, the spaces were filling up. More silhouettes gathered between the picnic tables and dunes.

He leaned away and took her by the hands. A car door slammed, and she started to turn. He took her by the chin. "It's just some tourists. But listen, while you're decompressing from the horror of these coins and what they represent—which I want you to put out of your mind—why don't we play a little game to cheer you up? We're going to have to go in a few minutes."

"Game?"

"One I made up—to get you into a positive frame of mind."

She shrugged and then nodded. "Okay."

"A little game of trivia. For every correct answer I'll owe you an ice cream cone."

"Well, that sounds pretty good."

In the meantime, Delia remained where she was along the fence. A second car door slammed. Coral started to turn, but once again, Matt distracted her. He reached around her left side to the circle of inverted scallop shells and picked one up, flipping it over to read the question written across its interior in Sharpie ink. "What is your favorite color?"

It was pink, of course.

"Now to earn each prize you must keep your eyes straight on me, even when I throw the question away. No turning around." He gave the shell a toss in the fence's direction and planted a kiss on Coral at the same time. "That's one ice cream."

"All right, the next question is going to be a little tougher." He picked up another shell. "What is your favorite boyfriend's name?"

She grinned as Matt formed an M with his lips, silently urging her to pronounce the word *Matt,* which she did. "Yes! Two ice creams. He kissed her and tossed the second shell away.

Several more questions followed.

By now, at the fence stood a long line of Matt's friends and family who had watched the entire scene, but Delia had disappeared.

Matt caught Coral as she tried to turn again and covered her eyes. "Nope. Ignore the tourist, Coral. Keep your eyes on me." He glanced at the fence and then returned his gaze to Coral. He uncovered her eyes. "Keep your focus on me," he reminded her once again and looked into those sapphire eyes.

She smiled, her mind clearly distracted now from the gold coins and their history.

"One more question, and then we'd better get going, okay?"

Coral grinned.

"Still love me?"

"Yes, I do."

"Correct, but the real question must come from the actual shell."

She glanced at the next one as he brought it around, a whelk this time instead of a scallop.

"Isn't that my—oh, don't throw that one away, Matt. Isn't that the one I found the gold coin in?"

"Correct. And—you get to keep this one—but only if you get the answer right."

She waited, grinning.

He held the shell. "Oh, wait. There's a scroll down inside." He pulled out the cylinder of pink paper and unrolled it.

"*Dear Coral,*" He looked into her sweet eyes, and then down at the paper again. "*I loved you from the moment I first saw you. There you were at the drink machines back at college, helping that poor guy in the wheelchair with his leg in the cast. Then you walked away with that flower in your hair, that pretty yellow dress, and your freckles—you were like the sunshine itself.*"

He glanced up to find tears in her eyes.

"Don't go doing that, now," he said, and continued.

"*And I was mesmerized. I had no idea who you were, but I had to know. I nicknamed you Sandy Beach—a name I later had to change and switched it to Sandy Shore. Who was this fine lady? So, I followed you to the building next door and raced upstairs in the library to watch for when you came out of class. School was nearly over, and I couldn't afford to miss you.*"

Coral pressed her fingers to her lips.

Matt lowered the scroll and placed the shell in her hand. "I was in love, Coral. And I still am." He wrapped her fingers around the shell. "Shake it now, Coral. Shake the shell."

Her eyes settled on his, and she lifted the shell to give it a jostle.

"Turn it over and shake harder. Your question's inside."

He watched as Coral gave the shell a little harder shake. A simple diamond ring landed on her skirt.

She gasped and took it in her fingers as she looked up at him.

He took her hands in his. "I've been working to buy it for you, Coral. The whole time we've been here." Then he shook his head. "I wasn't bored. I didn't need to help Grandma pay the rent. She's running over with money. But I wanted to do this myself. I knew from the start I couldn't imagine living life without you."

Coral tried to speak but he placed a finger over her lips. "Wait," he whispered. "And I want to know if you will have me. Will you marry me? That's the question."

She teared up. Nodded. "Yes, I will. Yes, yes, yes!"

He placed the ring on his angel's finger and not even the wild applause, cheers, and whistles from the parking-lot crowd could diminish their exuberant kiss.

41

After Matt's proposal I turned toward the applause to find a crowd lined up by the parking lot fence. My jaw dropped, and I stood to my feet, speechless. There stood Zeke, both grandmas, Jessica, Peter, Matt's mom and dad with Eddie, my dad, Millie, Larry and Jack, everybody. My tears kept rolling. I wondered how they'd kept so quiet.

Matt waved and hollered to the jubilant crowd. "She said yes!" He pumped his fist, "Whooo-eee! She told me yes!"

I laughed as I watched him and gathered my faculties enough to flash my diamond.

I'd never seen Matt so handsome as in that moment. I was so proud of him for all his creativity and the way he pulled this off. I had no idea.

He turned and grabbed up the towel, shook it off, and had me hold it while he heaved out the jug of gold. He made a sling with the towel and hung it over his shoulder while grabbing my hand. We headed into the crowd where all the ladies crowded around to admire my ring. Meanwhile, Matt ducked off to the side where Peter stood beside his car, and they locked the mayonnaise jar in its trunk.

Within minutes, the crowd dispersed to their vehicles, waving and saying things like, "We'll see you down at the *Princess*," or "See you in a few minutes." The parking lot cleared quickly, and Matt and I took off walking down the road.

Matt glanced at his watch. "We've got a few minutes," he said. "Let's visit the top of the bridge for old time's sake."

"What about that sunset event you mentioned? And why is everyone so dressed up? What's going on at the *Princess*?"

"Oh, you'll see! And by the way, did you know Jessica's grandfather is a justice of the peace?"

"Justice of the…Wait, now Matt…"

He laughed, "No, not us, Coral—not yet. Someone else."

Matt stood with Coral at the apex of the bridge. Below them in front of the restaurant sat Zeke's boat. Ralph and Zeke helped Grandma Allie and Grandma Rosella, both dressed in their finest, to climb into the vessel. A blonde, middle-aged lady in dark glasses and a sunhat followed behind. Her wildly flowered muumuu dress fluttered in the breeze as she stepped aboard. A Yorkie on a leash trotted at her side. Clusters of lavender roses, with large bows and matching streamers bedecked every available corner, post and railing. The florists must have emptied their fridges for this. Coral's father, fully handsome in his tux, greeted the women as they came aboard. On his elbow, in a sparkling silver gown, smiled Millie…and opposite the two of them stood Zeke in a fine white captain's uniform. Coral stared. "What in the world?"

"Your dad and Millie are getting married tonight, right at sunset."

She stood there agape. "So that's why you kept looking at your watch."

He nodded. "You can't imagine how nervous I was at the timing of all this."

"Didn't Millie want a courthouse wed—"

"That was your dad. But Millie wouldn't put up with it. She's a lot like you, Coral, with your designer's heart. And so," he motioned toward the *Gulf Princess*. "Here is their floating wedding chapel. Dinner, courtesy of Larry and Jack the dishwasher—who's learning pretty fast, they say—and dancing courtesy of some lovely CDs of waltzes and slow music—with décor arranged by Jessica."

"So that's why she's been so busy lately. I can't believe this day," Coral said. "I just cannot believe it."

"And look down there at the restaurant," he said. "See anything unusual?"

"What am I looking for? There's a *closed for repairs* notice is all."

"But what's the name on the sign?"

"It's Captain's…" She squinted at the restaurant's sign whose shape and color hadn't changed, only the lettering and her hand flew to her mouth. "Daddy's Place?

Matt laughed. "Yep. No more Captain's Table."

"Can I faint now?"

"And just to let you know, they weren't making repairs at the restaurant today," he said. "They were closed to prepare for the wedding."

Matt stood there admiring the rows of gleaming masts in the lowering sun, the sea gulls floating along, and the glint of the sun on the tiny waves. All the world was at peace.

He turned back to Coral and squeezed her hand and then lifted the ring to admire it. "Lovely," he said and kissed the back of her hand as he met her eyes. "But only because the most beautiful girl in the world is wearing it. And she's mine."

And there on the top of the bridge they kissed, the breeze blowing her hair across his face, and the low sun warming their skin. He leaned away and gazed into those blue eyes. Coral was his fiancée now.

"We'd better get down to Zeke's floating venue," he said. But as he turned, an old black car pulled to a stop at the crest of the bridge.

At the top of the bridge, I turned along with Matt as the car pulled to a slow stop.

I peered inside at the somewhat familiar face behind the wheel with her elbow out the window.

Matt beat me to a conclusion. "Delia?"

Could it be? With natural-colored hair.

The girl put on a sad smile and reached for an object in the passenger seat. She briefly lifted the all-too-recognizable blue wig and gave it a shake. "Yes, it's me, the same old Delia."

A long purple scar stretched from the top of her hairline to her right earlobe, but other than that, she was beautiful. No wonder she tried to cover it with the wig.

Delia sat there in the car as tears welled in her eyes. She leaned toward us and clutched the frame with her right hand. Her clumsy words fell over one another as she tried to make her point. "You know," she waved her fingers left and right, "up to now it's—it's been a kind of game—to me, anyway. But today I..."

I stood there in silence trying to figure what she was getting at. Matt remained silent.

Delia closed her eyes and sighed deeply. When she opened them again, she looked back at me. "Millie sat me down," she said, "and said some things..." Two fat tears rolled out of her eyes, and her voice cracked. "For one, she told me what you said..."

I searched for a response but nothing came.

Delia kept up her effort. "...that I'm no throw away, and Jesus made me spunky and smart in my own unique way."

"No, you're not a throw away..." I began.

"You don't know, I've been called trash all my life. But I wanna thank you..." She shook her head to regain her composure. "Sorry—my thoughts are all over the place..."

I bit my lips to keep from interrupting.

She continued. "And then Millie apologized to me." A note of incredulity warbled the girl's voice. "She apologized to *me*." A sob wracked her shoulders. She wiped her eyes and then her nose with the side of her hand. Then when nothing would come out, and mostly mouthing the words, she whispered, "Happy life." She leveled her gaze at me, and too choked to speak, she pointed at Matt first, and then to me and gave me a thumbs up, like a seal of approval.

Without another word or a backwards glance, she put her car back into drive, gave us a little parting wave, and pulled slowly down the other side of the bridge in the direction of Apalachicola.

I was dumbfounded. Matt and I stood there in silence and waved back.

Matt took Coral's hand, and they descended the bridge, circling the restaurant through the soft green grass. As they came back into view of the crowd on the *Gulf Princess,* he was forced to put all those musings on hold when renewed applause and cheers welcomed their boarding.

"All aboard!" Zeke said and closed the gate behind them with a grin and a wink. "Right on schedule and congratulations! Welcome aboard."

Matt gazed around at the guests and then announced Coral—officially. "Ladies and gentlemen, my fiancée Coral!"

More applause rose and then, with her at his elbow, they greeted each guest. Matt pointed at the young man with Sol and Paulette, "Eddie. Good to see you," he said. "Mom, Dad," he bent to hug them and realized they were holding hands. "Thank you for being here."

Mom and Dad seemed pleased with him. "Congratulations!" they said.

"I'm so glad you saw the proposal," Matt said.

"Wouldn't miss it," Dad said.

Mom reached out and squeezed Matt's fingers. "Your Coral's a lovely young lady, Son."

Behind him Larry and Jack stood at rear-stern, official protectors of the silver-topped buffet and wedding cake during the voyage. Matt and Coral greeted them, as well. The lady in the sunglasses was nowhere in sight, but Grandma Allie and Grandma Rosella sat portside, where Matt and Coral headed to give them hugs and find a seat. "Can we squeeze in next to you all?" he asked. The ladies made space, patting the seat for the two of them to sit down.

It seemed strange to be onboard and not be helping his friend Zeke, but the man had collared his old deckhand for the evening. Matt had never laid eyes on the guy before. But as he and Coral took their seats, Matt peeked up toward the cabin through the palms and flowers to catch a glimpse of the young man. Expecting to see fishing garb, he was surprised the deckhand also wore a clean white outfit.

And Matt did wonder about the little Yorkie dog in his arms.

The engines roared to life, and the *Princess* eased away from the dock. Matt sat back as the noise and the breeze consumed the ride.

Twenty minutes later, the *Gulf Princess* anchored off the coast of Carrabelle. A red sunset glowed like fire over the starboard side.

"See? look at the sunset," Matt said to Coral. "I was right."

"Like no other," she said. "And I will never forget it—or this day."

Sweet music, hidden earlier by the noise, now played clearly across the water, and Jessica's dad took his place as justice of the peace in front of the palms and flowers with Ralph. The cabin's Formica tables, normally shiny, were now bedecked in stretchy lavender covers and nosegays of roses.

Millie in her sparkles walked up the aisle to the tune of Canon in D Minor. After the *Do you, Ralphs, and the Do you, Millies*, Jessica's dad called on Grandma Rosella to come up and speak a blessing over the marriage. Before she prayed, Grandma explained the significance of doves in a wedding, symbols of peace, hope, new beginnings and the Holy Spirit in their marriage. Ralph and Millie then turned to a bamboo bird cage behind them. From behind the twin doors, they extracted two white doves and held the little creatures in cupped hands as Grandma prayed a blessing. As she finished, they released the birds. Applause was constrained, so as not to scare the doves as they found their way out the windows and fluttered into the distance together.

Matt leaned forward to see if Grandma Allie was thinking what he was thinking. "The doves. Remember the doves in your dream?" he said.

She gasped and folded her hands beneath her chin. A smile spread over her face, and her eyes met Matt's. They nodded.

He was the only one she'd confided in about that dream. He gave Allie's hand a pat. "It wasn't a bad omen after all. It was a good one." Thank God it came about in such a happy way.

After they set the birds free, Jessica's grandfather cleared his throat. "The groom may now kiss the bride," to which everyone cheered and clapped and whistled so loudly they could hardly hear the words that followed, "Ladies and gentlemen, I present to you Mr. and Mrs. Ralph Stone!"

A loud barrage of fireworks broke out from the top deck, its racket mixed with joyous music as the bride and groom ducked their way down the center of the boat to a silk-storm of flower petals and raucous approval and the barking of the little Yorkie up front with the deckhand.

As the new couple approached the buffet table, Millie stopped to toss her bridal bouquet. It flew back and hit Eddie in the head. To everyone's merriment his face reddened as he held the bouquet like a dead bug between his fingers. He passed the flowers to Paulette, Matt's mom, and that drew even more hilarity.

The deckhand passed the Yorkie to Zeke and scrambled upstairs, and the gaiety continued, accompanied by a full ten minutes more of fireworks from the upper deck.

Matt stepped aside with Coral as Ralph and Millie edged their way through the serving line where Larry and Jack stood behind the food warmers and served their plates. "Larry, young man," Ralph said, waving his hand across the wonderful buffet, "you're about to get a little more responsibility after this and a bit of a raise. And, Jack, you are too. We'll be needing a new dishwasher, so let's get the word out."

"Who set off those fireworks up top?" Millie asked.

Larry said nothing, just looked at Jack who shrugged.

"Oh, stop it, boys. Don't start that again. Who?"

Larry nodded in Jessica's direction. She stood next to the stairs beside her newly discovered grandfather as they gazed upstairs to the top deck. "You'll have to ask her," he said. "It's something about Jessica's mother—from Tallahassee. She came down to meet up with her father. Maybe she knows fireworks."

"Come on, now. You can do better than that, can't you?" Ralph said. "And did you boys even hear what I just told you? About the raise and so on?"

Larry saluted. "Yes sir."

Jack, wordless as usual, grinned and crossed his arms.

Matt and Coral stood in the buffet line behind Ralph and Millie who walked away with their plates, with Ralph mumbling something about the "cat's sure got that boy's tongue."

Then Ralph leaned toward Millie, "And I plan to be out on this boat a little more often. You comin' along?"

She laughed. "Maybe. If you can find me a new waitress."

Ralph chuckled, and they found a seat.

Matt and Coral filled their plates at the buffet and brought their plates to a table near the stairs. Jessica's mother had just climbed back down with the help of the deckhand. She now took off her sunhat and glasses and wrapped her arms around Jessie Sparrow, her own father.

Jessica had tears in her eyes, and Millie spoke up from the table next to Matt and Coral. "Everything okay with your grandfather?"

Jessica wiped her eyes and gave her a big smile. "Couldn't be better. These are happy tears." She gave Millie a thumbs-up before heading toward the buffet in the stern.

Millie elbowed Ralph. "You didn't answer me, dear."

"Absolutely, honey," he said, filling his mouth with buttered lobster. "I'll let the other waitress go first thing in the morning."

"Really?" Millie asked.

Ralph swallowed and took a sip from his glass. "Of course."

"I heard that," Matt said, leaning toward their table. "But I don't think you'll find it necessary."

Coral squeezed closer to Matt as Jessica joined their table. "Oh, sis," she said, "I can't believe you kept this wedding a secret! And this is what you've been up to. Just look at the *Gulf Princess!* She's so beautiful. You're good at this, sis. Really good."

Matt turned as Bobby Vinton's *Blue Velvet* kicked in, and his Mom and Dad rose to dance. They always did like that song.

Eddie rose to join their table and sat beside Jessica.

Matt watched as he gave a little bow and extended his hand. "May I have this dance?"

Jessica blushed and accepted. After the dance she leaned in toward Coral and Matt who were now finishing their plates. "I'll do you guys' wedding too. Have you picked a color?"

"Not yet," Coral said.

"But we'll be thinking about it," Matt added as they stood to the next tune, *Love is Blue.* "You just never know."

Epilogue

A few months after Dad and Millie's wedding, Dad and Matt sat me down at the restaurant. The look on their faces indicated a serious discussion. They'd become quite a team, and one mirrored the other.

"So, Coral," Matt began, "a little confession. Your dad and I have been holding back some news from you—only because we were concerned it might upset you. But now the time has come, and…"

Dad stepped in, "We'd like to drive you down to the Eastpoint Sheriff's Department so you can give them a DNA sample."

"Why would they need my DNA?" I frowned. "What do you mean?"

"Up at the campsite," Matt said. "There's been an investigation."

And then it registered. "They found a body?"

"Remember," Dad said, "when you and I and Jessica went out there? It was no bowl we found. It was a skull."

I gave him a nod. "Yeah, that was a little fishy," I said, "the way you two were acting."

Matt leaned forward and took my hand. "Turns out it was female."

"Hit in the head," Dad said, "Very suspect. They located an older male, too, under that fallen tree."

"You're kidding. I bet he killed her," I said. "Serves him right."

My dad shrugged. "At least he's not a danger anymore."

"You guys didn't need to worry about telling me that," I said. "But what about Grandma Allie?"

"If the body is Althea's," Matt said, "she will want to give her a proper burial,"

"You're right," I agreed. "She will."

The investigation ended by December, and we honored Althea with a proper burial in the same Carrabelle cemetery beside George Bentley, Grandma Allie's husband. I have no idea what the sheriff's department did with Horace Smith's bones. But blood relative or not, nobody wanted them in the family plot.

That fall Matt and I celebrated our own sunset wedding on the *Gulf Princess*. Jessica, who has since joined me in a part-time business she named Coastal Decorating, fulfilled her promise to decorate my pink and coral-themed wedding. It was a good match for the colors of the sunset. With Millie's help they festooned the vessel with satin ribbons, white daisies, coral and pink roses, and lots of baby's breath. Of course, Daddy's Place catered the event. Dad outdid himself as well as Larry and Jack. The weather was perfect, and the wedding could not have been more beautiful or the food more delicious.

"You should start a wedding business," I told Jessica.

That seed of an idea took root, and here we are three years later, with Jessica's new business Princess Weddings partnered with Coastal Decorating. Her engagement to Eddie, who now manages Sol's store out in Las Vegas, keeps them busy flying back and forth.

Larry now runs Daddy's Place. And now that Jack's been given the chance, he's turned out to be just as capable as Larry. The restaurant specializes in shark steaks and other seafood delights, and with all the new ocean-themed décor that Millie has added, it's become quite a destination for tourists and locals.

These days, with Larry in charge of Daddy's Place, my dad, the new owner and captain of *Gulf Prince*, a second charter boat of the Princess Fleet, doesn't have to worry much about the restaurant. Maybe it's because of a new development. When the boy's mother died shortly after Dad's marriage, Dad and Millie didn't hesitate to adopt him. And now I am happy to say I have a stepbrother.

Out on the boat recently, Zeke and I were chatting. "Your dad's a changed man," he said. "Thanks to you showing up, he's got his life back. And look at Millie, I've never met a more spoiled wife than her." His words melted my heart, and I thought about them for a long time.

Millie does work at the restaurant on occasion, but prefers going out on the boat with Dad. Along with Jessica and me, she helped Grandma Allie and Grandma Rosella spruce up the store.

With Matt's entrepreneurial help, its business has gained momentum. He's helped so many in town. Three years ago, with money borrowed from Sol he reinvented the vacant second floor over the restaurant. It now serves as several things—a wedding venue for the landlubbers with a stage behind the curtains for productions, the second floor Sock Hop Theatre where he plays old-timey movies with proper intermissions and very affordable popcorn and sodas. All the seats are moveable to make way for old-timey dances featuring music from the fifties and sixties.

The first thing we did was install an elevator of course so everyone, including the grandmas, can enjoy the festivities.

I sit in my favorite rocker, the one Matt fixed the squeak in, on the front porch of our tiny cottage behind Grandma Allie's store and think how I love my handsome industrious man. He's so full of ideas.

Then my phone rings. It's Matt himself. "Dad's on the way down to Florida," he says. "With Mom, of course. He said don't buy anything for the twins; they're bringing a carload of toys for them."

Our babies, Rosella and Allie, have just begun to walk. Sol and Paulette, who married a few days after Dad and Millie, have made so many trips down here to spoil the kids they might as well move on down. I caress my protruding belly, where our newest addition is beginning to show. It's a boy, the doctor says.

Matt clears his voice on the phone, and I think I know what's coming.

"Do we have room to put up Eddie too?"

I laugh. "Of course, we do." If we don't have room in our tiny cottage then somebody else will.

Tears well up in my eyes. God has multiplied my blessings. Sometimes I'm overwhelmed at His grace. Like the Good Book says, He truly does *set the solitary in families*.

Acknowledgements

Special thanks to Thomas Riley, librarian at the Carrabelle Branch of Franklin County, and for his assistance and information. Thank you, Stephen Caraher, RN, for your injury advice, and to Major Dwayne Coulter, Eastpoint, Florida, Sheriff's Department for jurisdictional and procedural information. Many thanks to Katherine Medina Forensic Crime Scene Supervisor of the Marion County, Florida, Sheriff's Department for foundational advice on crime scene procedures. Heartfelt thanks go to Larry Chauncey of Silver City in Ocala, Florida for his information on gold coins and jewelry-making. Thanks to the members of my local Word Weavers International chapter for their helpful advice and careful critiques. Thank you to my special beta readers, Chuck and Delores Kight, Mary Busha, Katherine Medina, and to my family for all their patience. Note that any and all errors are my own.

About the Author

Jennifer Odom is a 5th generation Floridian. Her love of the land and its rich history reach back to the 1860s when her great great grandfather migrated to his new homestead in Central Florida near the railroad. Orange groves and farming busied the family while one child and her spouse established the general store and served as station-master for the thriving depot. Reflecting this love of Florida and its people, Jennifer has written human interest stories for the *Ocala Star Banner* and gardening articles for the *Ocala Gazette*. Her fiction is published in *Splickety* and *Clubhouse Jr.* magazines, as well as *Maine Review's Juxtaposition.* Her fifth novel, *Along the Forgotten Coast,* is the second volume in her heart-warming *Coral Series* and serves as the satisfying sequel to *Under the Mango Trees.* Her *Black Series* (suspense/mystery) includes *Summer on the Black Suwannee, Stranger with a Black Case,* and *Girl with a Black Soul.*

Jennifer is a multi-award winning veteran teacher and writer, selected as Teacher of the Year at her Florida Blue Ribbon School, and Writer of the Year at the Florida Christian Writers Conference. Connect with Jennifer online at:

jenniferodom.com

www.ingramcontent.com/pod-product-compliance
Lightning Source LLC
Chambersburg PA
CBHW020759310726

48969CB00002B/621